A KISS, A DANCE & A DIAMOND

HELEN LACEY

MILLS & BOON

First Published in Great Britain 2018
by Mills & Boon, an imprint of HarperCollins*Publishers*
1 London Bridge Street, London, SE1 9GF

A Kiss, a Dance & a Diamond © 2018 Helen Lacey

ISBN: 978-0-263-26489-0

38-0418

MIX
Paper from
responsible sources
FSC™ C007454

This book is produced from independently certified FSC™ paper to ensure responsible forest management.

For more information visit: www.harpercollins.co.uk/green

Printed and bound in Spain
by CPI, Barcelona

For Gareth and Stephen.
Because big brothers are the best.

Chapter One

Kieran O'Sullivan was home.

For good.

He rubbed the back of his neck, stretched out his spine and figured he should down another cup of coffee since he had three hours to go before the end of his double shift. It had been a busier-than-usual afternoon in the ER at the Cedar River Community Hospital, but nothing like he'd been used to when he'd lived and worked in Sioux Falls. Still, he'd treated two minor burns, a dislocated shoulder, a baby with a bad case of croup and a teenager who'd fractured her arm after falling off a horse.

He was five days into his new job at the hospital.

Five days of unpacking boxes and settling into the apartment he'd rented.

Five days pretending life was sweet.

And five days that he'd managed to avoid running into Nicola Radici.

He ignored the twinge in his gut and the way the word *coward* mashed its way into his thoughts. Because it wasn't as though he hadn't seen Nicola or spoken to her in the past twelve months. He had. Several times.

But this was different. He was now back in Cedar River for good. Back in the town where he'd been born and raised—a town of a few thousand that sat in the shadow of the Black Hills, South Dakota.

Yeah, back home for good with no way of avoiding her.

High school sweethearts.

The damned phrase still made him cringe.

It had been fifteen years since they'd spectacularly broken up after graduation. Since then he'd married and divorced, and he knew Nicola had a broken engagement in her past…so there was no logical reason he should have any feelings about her one way or another.

But he did.

He had guilt.

By the bucket load.

For over a decade and a half, he'd regularly returned to Cedar River to visit his family. But he'd usually managed to avoid running into her. She'd moved to San Francisco, gone to college, gotten a life that didn't include him…just as he'd told her to do. While he'd gone to college and med school, ending up at the largest hospital in Sioux Falls. That was where he met Tori, who soon became his wife and the mother of his son. Everything had worked out as he'd imagined it would.

Until it blew up in his face.

Kieran shook the memory off, hating that after nearly two years he still had the same aching loss seeping into his bones. Nothing eased it. And he suspected nothing ever would. But he had to pretend he was over the whole awful mess. He had a job, parents, siblings, friends… too many things and people eclipsing his grief to behave as broken inside as he felt. It was better to simply make out he was okay.

And he was, most of the time. But since he'd made the decision to move back to Cedar River a few months back and secured a permanent position at the hospital, a peculiar uneasiness had simmered in his gut. And he suspected it had nothing to do with returning home for good, nothing to do with the fact that his parents were divorcing or that months earlier he'd discovered he had a secret half brother who lived in Portland, a product of his father's thirty-year-old infidelity.

No, it wasn't anything to do with that. It had everything to do with Nicola Radici.

Because Nicola, with her long brown hair and dark eyes, was as sensational now as she'd been in high school.

And because she still clearly hated the sight of him.

Every time they'd spoken in the past twelve months, like at his brother Liam's wedding a few months back, she'd tilted her chin, pushed back her shoulders and offered a cursory response when he'd said hello and asked how she was. Even when he'd offered his condolences to her and her family over the loss of her brother, Gino, who'd been tragically killed in a boating accident eighteen months ago. He knew how she felt, since he'd lost his sister Liz three years earlier.

Kieran recognized the lingering resentment in her expression.

She hadn't forgiven him for humiliating her so many years ago.

Not that he blamed her. He had broken up with her on graduation day, just outside her locker, right in front of the whole school. He hadn't meant to do it that way, but it had happened regardless.

Kieran shook off the memory and headed for the doctor's lounge to grab a much-needed cup of coffee.

Just as he was taking a sip, one of the nurses poked her head around the door.

"Dr. O'Sullivan," she said and waved an admission folder. "There's a patient in triage, bed three. A young boy with a fish hook in his hand."

Kieran spilled the rest of the coffee down the sink and rinsed out the mug. "Okay, I'll be right there."

The nurse hovered by the doorway and gave a kind of uneasy shrug. "Um…it's one of the Radici boys."

His stomach plummeted. Particularly when he saw the nurse's expression. His old relationship with Nicola wasn't exactly a secret, and many of the nurses, including the fiftysomething woman in front of him, had lived in Cedar River all their lives. And since his family was the wealthiest and most high profile in town, gossip came with the territory. But damn, the last thing he wanted was to see Nicola, especially when he'd just been thinking about her.

"He's a patient, so it's not a problem," he said anyway, heading toward triage.

He spotted Nicola immediately, standing beside one of the beds, the privacy curtain half-pulled around. Dressed in jeans, a bright red shirt, ankle boots and with a blue sweater wrapped around her waist, she was effortlessly attractive. Her hair was loose—her wild, curly dark brown hair that hung down her back and had always driven him crazy—and he was suddenly overcome by the memory of the two of them in the back of his Wrangler, going all the way when they were sixteen and losing their virginity together.

Then, he quickly pushed the memory away and kept walking.

There was a dark-haired boy standing at her side, his arms crossed, and another, younger child sitting on the edge of the bed. Her nephews. It was common knowledge that she'd inherited custody of her brother's two kids upon his death. Kieran took a breath, put on his best physician's face and walked towards them.

"Nicola," he said quietly. "Hello."

She turned her head and met his gaze. The resentment was still there, burning bright in her lush brown eyes. He saw the pulse in her throat beating wildly as she spoke. "Dr. O'Sullivan."

Nothing else. There was no welcome in her voice. Nothing other than cool resentment. And the way she called him *doctor* made that resentment abundantly clear.

He plastered a smile on his face. "It's good to see you, Nic."

Big mistake. She clearly didn't want to be reminded of the way he used to call her *Nic* because she glared at him, pressing her lips together. Kieran watched as she swallowed hard, with her arms crossed so tightly they might snap.

One of her steeply arched eyebrows rose a fraction. "I thought Dr. Wright was on duty tonight?"

Of course. She wouldn't have come to the ER if she suspected Kieran would be there. And she obviously knew he'd started working at the hospital. News traveled fast in Cedar River. Kieran half shrugged. "She'll be here later," he explained and moved around the bed. "I'm on a double shift because we're down a doctor this week. I finish up in three hours." He felt her scrutiny down to his bones. "So...let's see what's going on with your nephew's hand," he said, getting the conversation back on track.

"I hooked myself," the child on the bed muttered,

holding up his clumsily bandaged hand, his eyes downcast. "See?"

"He was messing around," the older boy said and looked toward his aunt. "I told him to stop."

"I was not!" his brother said hotly and waved his hand and then yelped in pain. "You said I couldn't cast my line and you kept laughing."

"You were casting like a girl," the older Radici brother said. "And into a bucket in the backyard. That's not even real casting. You can't do anything."

"I can so!"

"You're such a baby," the older boy said.

Kieran looked at Nicola and saw that she was frowning.

"Johnny," she scolded. "Please don't make things worse."

The older boy had a scowl so deep it creased his forehead. He shrugged. "I'm gonna sit over there."

Kieran smiled to himself. It would be exactly the same conversation he might once have had with his own brothers when they were kids. He watched as Johnny shuffled sulkily across the triage zone and plunked into a chair, then took a gaming console out of his small backpack, shoved plugs into his ears and ignored all of them.

Kieran looked at the younger child. "You know, when we were kids, my brother Liam always said I couldn't fish as well as he could. I was younger, and my arms weren't as long as his. But you know what? I grew up taller than him."

The boy looked at him for the first time and his eyes widened. "You did?"

"Yep," Kieran replied and grinned. "And now I'm a way better fisherman than he is."

"Really?" he asked, looking pensive.

"Really," Kieran assured him.

The boy shrugged. "It's not really fishing. It's just a bucket and some plastic toys."

"Well," Kieran said as he moved around the bed and dropped the clipboard onto it. "Maybe you'll get so good you can do it for real sometime."

Kieran saw a kind of wary panic cross the child's face, and he looked quickly toward Nicola. She glanced sideways, and he saw her shake her head slightly. He sensed something was wrong but didn't comment further. Instead, he washed his hands in the sink, pulled on a pair of gloves and then gently placed the boy's wrapped hand on a small rolling table. "Okay, let's see what you've done. First, though, you better tell me your name."

"Marco," he muttered, his lip wobbling.

"Okay, Marco," Kieran said and began to unwrap the makeshift bandage. "Let's do this."

The boy whimpered a little, calming when Nicola moved forward and grasped his other hand. Kieran tried not to think about how it was the closest he'd been to her in fifteen years. Or about how he could pick up the scent of her vanilla shampoo over the antiseptic that usually lingered in the air. The scent was suddenly so familiar it made him glance sideways.

She wasn't looking at him, though. Her attention was focused solely on her nephew.

He could see how she was slightly biting her bottom lip and remembered how she used to do that when she was deep in thought, like when they'd been studying together back in high school. Of course, studying usually turned into making out, which often led to more. Back then he'd been crazy for her, mad for her beautiful hair, sexy curves and warm brown eyes. A typical horny teenage boy who couldn't get enough of his first real girlfriend. Back then, in the three years they'd dated, Kieran was sure he and Nicola would go the distance, that they'd go to college, travel the world, get married one day, have a family. But that was a kid's dream. Because the moment Nicola had suggested they get engaged before they headed off to college, he'd freaked out. He'd felt trapped and afraid that settling down so young would derail his career. And he'd never quite forgiven himself for hurting her the way he had.

And, clearly, she hadn't, either.

There were tears in Marco's eyes, and Kieran focused his attention on the child. He was a quiet sort of kid, clearly in pain, but trying to be brave. "You know, if you want to say *ouchywowah*, you can."

The child's eyes widened. "Ouchy, what?"

"Ouchywowah," Kieran said and finished unwrapping the bandage. "Saying it three times helps make the pain go away. But you have to say it quietly," he explained, not daring to look at Nicola. "Like, in a whisper…or it doesn't work."

"Really?"

"Really," Kieran assured him and smiled to himself as the boy began chanting the word over and over. Silly as it was, it seemed to help Marco concentrate on something other than his injury and, ten minutes later, Kieran had removed the fishing hook impaled between Marco's fingers, cleaned and stitched the injury and ordered some pain medication. He left the nurse to dress the young boy's hand, while he did something he didn't want to do: speak to Nicola—alone.

"I've arranged for a scrip for some painkillers you can fill at the hospital pharmacy, and I'd like to see him again in a few days, to make sure he's free from infection," he explained as they walked through triage, away from the two boys and through to the waiting room outside.

Other than her nephews, the nurse on duty in triage and a couple of nurses in the reception area, the place was empty, and Kieran experienced a sudden and acute sense of discomfort. They were, in a sense, alone for the first time in fifteen years.

And he could tell by the look in her brown eyes that he was about to get the telling off he figured was a decade and a half in the making...

Don't do it...

Nicola chanted the words to herself over and over. She didn't want to make a scene. She didn't want to spend any more time in Kieran O'Sullivan's presence. But damn, it was hard. He was still too gorgeous for words...six foot two and a half, broad shoulders, brownish-blond hair that still flopped over his forehead when he tilted his head, glittering blue eyes and dark lashes. And the whiskery shadow across his jaw was too attractive for words. Not exactly a beard, but enough to give him a kind of rugged sexiness. She wished he'd grown up to be bald and pudgy. She wished he hadn't decided to permanently return to Cedar River. She wished he hadn't been so kind and considerate with Marco and that her nephew hadn't actually responded to him—which was way more than he did with most people. She wished a whole lot of things. And in that moment she wished she could turn on her heels and leave the hospital as quickly as she could.

But she couldn't.

She had Johnny and Marco to think about.

A deep surge of grief coursed through her entire body when she thought about her older brother, Gino, and sister-in-law, Miranda. She loved her nephews but worried she wasn't measuring up in the parent department. And along with running the restaurant and her father's swiftly declining health, she had enough on her plate without adding an old boyfriend into the mix.

But...she was mad.

Seething.

Kieran O'Sullivan had no right coming back to town! He'd set the rules on graduation day. He wanted a life and a career away from Cedar River. He didn't want any ties. He didn't want a girlfriend. He didn't want to get engaged. He wanted to be able to screw around in college. He wanted his freedom.

She should have seen it coming. In the weeks before graduation, he'd been distant and closed off and had avoided her like the plague. Ever since she'd suggested they make a real commitment to one another before heading off to separate colleges. And then, on graduation day, he'd dumped her, saying he didn't want to be tied down...by her or Cedar River.

But now he was back.

And suddenly, all her pent-up rage, despair and resentment was pointing in one direction. And even though she knew that being angry was illogical after so many years, she couldn't help it.

"You're a real jerk," she said and waved her hands. "You know that? Why did you have to come back? *Egoista, bastardo di cuore freddo!*" she cursed in Italian, feeling her skin heat more with each passing second and fighting the urge to take a swipe at his handsome face. *"Ti odio!"*

I hate you...

They were strong words, and she knew he understood them. But he didn't flinch. Didn't speak. Didn't do anything other than take her ranting at him as though he'd been expecting it. And that amplified her anger tenfold. She didn't want him to be compliant and agreeable and ready for her insults. She wanted him to respond so she could go in for another round. And another. Until she was spent and done with all the pain she still harbored from her broken, seventeen-year-old-girl's heart.

"I know," he said quietly. "I'm sorry."

Nicola tilted her chin. "Your apology is about fifteen years too late."

"I know that, too."

Nicola drew in a sharp breath. Typical of Kieran to be so damned agreeable! "I'll take Marco to our usual doctor," she said flatly. "That way I won't have to see you again."

"If that's what you'd prefer."

God, he was so compliant. "I think we both know what I'd prefer, *Doctor.*"

"That I'd stayed away?"

"Exactly."

"It's my hometown, Nicola…just as much as it is yours. And I'm pretty sure it's big enough for both of us."

Nicola glanced around, arms crossed, temper surging. "It doesn't feel like it right now." She sucked in a long and steadying breath. "However, I do appreciate you looking after him tonight."

She wasn't about to tell him that it was the first time she'd seen Marco really respond to someone new since his parents had been killed. And of course she wasn't surprised that Kieran had a great bedside manner. He'd always been too damned charming for his own good!

"We don't have to be friends, Nicola," he said evenly. "But we don't have to be enemies, either."

"I don't want us to be *anything*," she shot back. "Except strangers."

"You're my sister-in-law's friend," he reminded her. "This is a small town, and we're bound to run into one another occasionally. I prefer we weren't at war when we did."

He was right. Her longtime friend Kayla had married Kieran's brother, and they'd just had their first child. They would definitely cross paths.

But she resented that he was so cool, so logical…so incredibly infuriating about the whole situation.

A typical O'Sullivan trait. They were the wealthiest family in town. And the most entitled. They owned commercial and investment property and several businesses, including the hugely successful O'Sullivan's Hotel. The eldest brother, Liam, ran the hotel and most of the other holdings, while the younger brother Sean was a movie and music producer in LA. Their sister, Liz, had passed away a few years earlier from some kind of heart thing, leaving behind three young daughters. And there was another brother, too, called Jonah, who they'd just discovered existed and was the reason his parents were now in the middle of a divorce.

And then there was Kieran—the brother who'd left to pursue his dream of a medical career. And he'd got exactly what he wanted. He was smart and charming and too good-looking for words. He'd once been her closest friend, her lover, her future. Now, all she felt was hurt and rage when she thought of him. Nicola tried to wrap up her temper and put it away where it belonged. But it was so *hard*.

Pull yourself together. He's not worth it.

"Can we go now?"

Johnny's voice. Jerking her back into the land of good sense and logic.

Nicola crossed her arms and moved quickly toward him. "Of course," she said to her nephew. She glanced briefly toward Kieran. "Thank you for your help."

She didn't look at him again as she walked back into triage, quickly ushering both boys back through the corridor. And did her best to ignore Kieran. But he watched her. She could feel his gaze burning through her as she left. She made a quick stop at the pharmacy to fill the painkiller prescription and then headed home, her thoughts consumed by the last person she wanted to think about.

She was embarrassed that she'd lost her temper. But, hell and damnation, he pushed her buttons! He always had. In high school she'd been desperately in love with him.

After graduation day, she'd hated him.

That rage and anger had kept her going, made her stronger, gave her the strength to leave town and pursue her dreams. She'd headed to California and attended college in San Francisco, studied hard and graduated with a degree and a burning desire to climb the corporate ladder. Six years later, she was head of human resources at an organic food company. That was where she'd met Carl. He was the managing director of the East Coast division. He was smart and good-looking and recently divorced. They'd had a whirlwind romance. Despite her friends warning her she was his rebound relationship, within a year they'd bought a house, an engagement ring and made plans for the future. But three months later he left, claiming he still had feelings for his ex-wife. The house was sold and she quickly returned the ring.

Broken and hurt, Nicola had learned a valuable lesson—she was never going to be anyone's rebound girl again.

"Aunt Nicola," Marco said as they drove back through town, "can we have gelato when we get home?"

She glanced at the clock on the dash. It was seven o'clock, a little late for her nephew's favorite treat. "Tomorrow," she promised. "I'll get *Nonno* to make your favorite strawberry flavor, okay?"

Despite his declining health, her father still insisted on making the gelato that JoJo's was famous for. The pizzeria had been in her family for over forty years, since her grandfather had started the place a decade after he'd arrived in Cedar River. Back then, he'd planned on making a fortune mining silver, but instead Guido and Josephine Radici had turned their hands to doing what they did best—cooking the most authentic Italian cuisine this side of the Black Hills. And it was a family business in the truest sense of the word. Her father, Salvatore, had learned the business from his father and continued on alone after her mother's death a few years earlier. Her late brother Gino had learned from their dad. Although she missed her mother, Nicola was glad her mom hadn't had to endure Gino's passing. It was bad enough watching her father slowly deteriorate through his grief at the loss of his beloved son, along with a series of minor strokes. And since her older brother Vince had moved to San Francisco years ago, now there was just her…trying to cobble together some sense of normalcy for Gino's two sons.

But it wasn't easy. With Marco's emotional withdrawal and Johnny's penchant for getting into trouble, she had her hands full. Both boys grieved in their own way, but it was Marco who really concerned her. He suffered from night terrors and had developed a severe fear of water. Although neither of the boys were with their parents at the time of the accident, the fact they were killed while sailing had profoundly affected Marco, and now he refused to go near water except for a quick shower at bath time. He'd always loved fishing but now resorted to hooking plastic toys from a bucket in the backyard.

Once they were back home, Nicola parked the car, grabbed her tote and ushered the boys from the back seat. The house was where the boys had always lived— Gino and Miranda's home, which they'd bought when they got married. It was a few minutes out of town, on a wide, tree-lined street, with a swing set in the backyard and a porch out front. After her brother's death, Nicola had quickly packed up her life in San Francisco and moved in, trying to keep the boys' normal routine as smooth as possible—soccer on Saturdays, joining a couple of other parents in a carpool for school pick-up twice a week, family night on a Friday with a movie and popcorn in the rooms behind the restaurant. She even did her best to pack the same kind of lunches that their mother had each morning.

Her friend Annie Jamison was a nanny to three children, and she'd counselled Nicola to maintain as much of their old routine as possible to encourage emotional stability in the wake of their grief and loss. So she did. Normality was the key.

Even though, some days, she felt as though every moment was an uphill battle.

And tonight, she discovered about an hour later, was becoming one of those battles.

Johnny wanted to stay up late to play a computer game, and Marco refused to go to bed and was holed up in his room, hiding in the corner of his closet, rejecting her requests to come out even when she relented and offered him the gelato he'd asked for earlier.

"Please come out," she pleaded, standing by the closet door, knowing she could wrestle him out of the small space, but she didn't want to upset him any more than he already was.

Yeah…an uphill battle just about covered it.

"No," he wailed. "You don't care what happens to me."

Nicola hung on to patience and remained by the door. "Of course I do. Please, Marco…it's nearly bedtime. You have to get up for school in the morning."

"I'm not going back to that stupid school!"

She sucked in a long breath. "Marco, please—"

"Everyone's hates me. And my hand hurts," he wailed. "No one is nice to me. Not you. Not Johnny. No one except that doctor."

Except that doctor.

Nicola's breath stilled in her chest. *Kieran.* She tried to ignore the way her pulse started to beat wildly. "Well, he's not here. He's at the hospital, and you don't need to be there now. But I'm here, and I'd really like to talk to you. So, can you come out, and we'll have some gelato and spend some time together…okay?"

Silence. The deafening kind. She heard movement and thought she'd made progress when he spoke again. "You could call him. Doctors come to people's houses, too."

Nicola hung on to her patience and took a deep breath. "I can't do that."

She heard him huff. "You never do *anything* I want. Only what Johnny wants."

The pain in his voice was unmistakable. The boys had once been close, but over the past few months she'd seen the divide between them become wider.

The guilt landed squarely on her shoulders. She was a lousy parent. And she clearly needed help.

Nicola left the room and headed downstairs. She got to the living room and discovered the overhead light bulb had blown. *Great...that's all I need.* She loathed heights and had no intention of bothering her neighbor for a ladder, even though she was sure the elderly man would help if she asked. Besides, her independent streak made her resist asking anyone for assistance. But as she got to the kitchen, filled the kettle and sat down at the table, Nicola admitted that she did need help. Right now.

A minute later she was calling the hospital, feeling foolish through to her bones. He'd probably left for the night, and she hoped he had. She didn't want to talk to him. She didn't want to ask for his help. But within seconds she was connected to the ER, and a moment later she heard his deep voice.

"O'Sullivan," he said as a greeting.

She clenched the phone and sucked in a sharp breath. "Kieran..."

Silence stretched like brittle elastic, and then he spoke again. "Nicola? Is that you?"

She was shocked that he'd recognized her voice. "I... I..."

"Is everything okay?"

Her belly did a foolish loop-the-loop at the concern in his voice, and then words just blurted out. "Kieran... I need you."

Chapter Two

Twenty minutes later Kieran was pulling up outside a two-story home on Grove Street.

I need you...

It had been fifteen years since he'd heard Nicola say anything so provocative.

He glanced at the address scribbled on a crumpled note on the passenger seat and saw that he had the right place. It was ironic that she lived only a couple of streets from the apartment he'd rented. The large Victorian he'd moved into five days earlier had been divided into several apartments, and his was on the second floor. His sister-in-law, Kayla, had been the previous tenant so it had been an easy sublet, taking over the payments and dealing with the landlord. And he liked the place well enough. There was one bedroom, a combined kitchen and dining room, and a spacious living room—plenty of room for the few boxes and sparse assortment of furniture he'd brought with him from Sioux Falls.

He got out, locked the Jeep and headed for the house. The porch light flicked on the moment he closed the white picket gate, and within seconds the front door opened. Once he was up the three steps and on the porch, Nicola was there, holding the screen door open and inviting him inside.

"Thank you for coming," she said quickly as he crossed the threshold and she closed the door. "I know it's late and you've been working and I shouldn't have called but he was asking for you and I didn't—"

"Nicola," he said, cutting her off as he followed her down the hall. "Slow down, you're rambling."

She stopped and turned to face him. God, she was beautiful. His blood suddenly rumbled in his veins, and an old attraction spectacularly resurfaced, knocking him out. And in that moment he realized nothing had changed. He was still as attracted to Nicola as he'd always been.

But he would never let her know it. There was no point. They were ancient history, and he was in no condition to get involved with anyone. Particularly a woman who clearly hated the sight of him.

"Rambling?" she echoed, glaring at him.

He nodded, biting back a grin. "Yeah…rambling. Take a breath and calm down."

"I am calm," she shot back. "I've just had a crappy day. We'll have to go to the kitchen as the light bulb in the living room has blown."

He glanced into the darkened room as they passed. "Want me to fix it?"

"No," she said and kept walking.

"So, what seems to be the problem?"

"I can't get Marco out of the closet," she said and then quickly explained how the boy liked to hide there. "And when he asked to see you, I just… I couldn't think of anything else to do except call. He doesn't generally take to strangers…which is good, I suppose. But he seemed to connect with you at the hospital, and all I could do was what he asked. Right now, I simply want him to come out of the closet and get some sleep. Plus, he said his hand hurts."

"He's got a few stitches, so that's not unusual," Kieran said, realizing she was clearly frazzled and holding on by a thread. "I'll talk to him in a minute, but perhaps you should fill me in on what's been going on with him lately."

She nodded. "Sure."

Kieran followed her up the hall. "Where's your other nephew?"

"Bed. Johnny fights to stay up and play video games and then ends up flaked out on the floor in his room," she said as they entered the kitchen. "He's willful and defiant and doesn't do anything I say. Unlike Marco, who is usually a people pleaser and hates getting into trouble. But tonight… I think he's simply overwhelmed by his injury and after what happened at school…" She sighed and her voice trailed off. "It's been one of those days."

"What happened at school?" he asked, standing on the other side of the island. watching as she began pouring coffee into two mugs.

"He got bullied today," she explained quietly. "And then he got upset, and some of his classmates saw, and then he withdrew like he sometimes does and wouldn't talk to his teacher. It's happened before. I left the restaurant, picked him up early and brought him home. But he still wouldn't talk to me. I didn't even know he'd hurt himself on the fishing hook until I called him in for dinner. He'd wrapped a T-shirt around his hand so I wouldn't know."

Kieran considered her words. "Have you thought about getting him to talk with a professional?" he asked quietly. "He's obviously having trouble coping with the death of his parents, and naturally so, but I could make a few inquiries and find someone who works specifically with children if you would like a referral."

She nodded fractionally. "It may come to that. But for now, I'd just like to get him out of the closet."

"Sure," he said and noticed that her hands were shaking a little. "Does he have nightmares?"

"Yes," she replied and pushed the mug across the counter. "I have cream and sugar."

"This is fine," he said and took the mug. One brow rose. "Your tastes have changed."

He met her gaze. "Some," he said and tried to ignore the way his heart beat faster than usual. "So, about his nightmares…does he talk to you about them?"

"Sometimes. He has a fear of water," she said and sipped her coffee. "That's why he fishes out of a bucket."

Kieran recalled that her brother and sister-in-law lost their lives in a boating accident and how Marco had responded at the hospital when he'd mentioned he might want to try fishing for real. "Because of his parents' accident?"

"Yes," she replied softly. "The boys weren't with them that day. It was just pure luck, really. They'd both had head colds and my sister-in-law Miranda didn't want to risk them getting worse," she explained.

"Gino and Miranda were good people," Kieran said. "I used to stop by JoJo's sometimes, when I'd come home to visit my folks. As I recall, they were dedicated sailors."

She nodded. "They competed in all the major events. They were in San Francisco for the regatta, which they did every year. I loved it because it meant Vince and I could see them, and we could catch up as a family."

Kieran knew Vince had moved to San Francisco straight out of high school. It was one of the reasons Nicola had chosen to go to college there, to be close to her older brother.

"Vince has a big apartment in the city," she explained quietly. "And they always stayed with him when they were there. I was at my brother's apartment watching the kids because Gino and Miranda had gone for a sail outside the bay before the races started the next day. They say the storm came out of nowhere." She sighed and shrugged. "I don't know... Gino was always so careful about the dangers of doing what he loved. But on that day, he miscalculated. It was days before their bodies were found...but by then we knew something terrible had happened. Vince identified them, and then we had to tell the boys. It was the hardest thing I have ever done."

Kieran watched as her eyes glittered with tears and she blinked a couple of times. There was something incredibly vulnerable about her in that moment, and he fought the sudden urge to reach across and touch her. Comforting Nicola was out of the question. He had to remember that. She wasn't a patient or a friend. She was the girl he'd loved in high school. She was his past. End of story.

"You know," he said and met her gaze, "I've seen fear manifest from loss before...it's not uncommon, particularly in a child. In time, and with patience and maybe therapy, he'll probably overcome his fears."

"I hope so," she said quietly. "Until then, I have to work out how to make him feel safe. Unfortunately, I feel as though I'm failing at every turn."

It was quite an admission, and one he was sure she hadn't intended divulging. Hours ago, she'd made her feelings toward him abundantly clear—she still hated him. And yet now he was standing in her kitchen, listening to her earnest words, drinking coffee and acting as though it was all absurdly normal.

"I'm sure you're not," he assured her. "Parenting is a challenge even in the best of circumstances."

"You'd know more about that than me."

A familiar ache hit him directly in the center of his chest, and he quickly averted his gaze. He didn't want to see her eyes, didn't want to speculate as to how much she knew about him and his life before he'd returned to Cedar River. But people talked. He knew that. But with everything else that was going on with his family—with his parents' impending divorce, the discovery of his half brother, and then his other brother Liam secretly marrying the daughter of their father's sworn enemy, he hoped that his own smashed-up personal life might not rate a mention on the radar. But when he did finally glance at her again, he figured that she knew enough. Maybe not everything, particularly how broken up inside he felt most of the time, but she certainly had some idea of what he'd been through.

"Later," he said and shrugged. "You can ask me later."

She shrugged loosely. "I shouldn't have said that. Your private life is none of my business."

He nodded. "Anyway, for now, we should probably go and talk with Marco."

She placed her mug on the counter. "He's upstairs."

He followed her from the kitchen and up the stairway, trying not to notice how her hips swayed as she walked. Or the way her perfume assailed his senses. Other than in a professional capacity, it had been a long time since he'd been so close to a woman. He hadn't been intimate with anyone since he'd separated from Tori. Casual sex had never been his thing, and he wasn't interested in a committed relationship, so the best thing was to avoid women altogether until he worked through his demons. But he hadn't figured on his old attraction for Nicola making a comeback.

Get a grip, O'Sullivan...

Ten minutes later, he still hadn't managed to coax Marco from his hiding spot in the closet, but the child was at least answering him. To his credit, he'd made the tiny space into a fort, complete with walls and windows, out of several old cardboard boxes and several towels pegged together. Looking at how he'd used his imagination allayed some of his concerns for the boy's emotional well-being. This was clearly Marco's safe place, his go-to spot when he felt cornered or unhappy or despairing. Kieran wasn't an expert in child psychology, but he was relieved to discover that Marco wasn't simply hiding in a confined space staring at the wall.

"You've built a really cool fort," Kieran said quietly.

Marco was silent, then grunted. "Johnny says it's lame."

"Well, I'm something of an expert at fort building," he said, flicking his gaze toward Nicola, who stood in the doorway. He caught a tiny smile at the edges of her mouth and ignored the way it made his gut churn. "When my brothers and I were young, we turned our treehouse into a fort. It had a moat, too."

He heard a shuffling sound, like sneakers shifting across carpet, and then spotted Marco peering around the door frame.

"A moat?" the boy asked. "Really?"

"Yeah," Kieran replied. "It had water in it, too. I fell into it once and dislocated my collarbone."

Marco's eyes widened, and he stepped out of the closet. "That must have hurt a lot."

"It did," he said and nodded. "So, your aunt said your hand was hurting."

"Yeah," the boy said, his voice cracking.

"On a scale of one to ten, how much does it hurt?" Kieran asked.

"Ten," Marco replied quickly.

Kieran glanced at Nicola, saw the concern on her face and offered a reassuring nod. "Ten," he mused. "Really? That's a lot. Are you sure?"

Marco's bottom lip wobbled. "Well…maybe a five."

"Five… I see. Then, that's not so bad, right? Remember the word I said you need to say over and over?"

The boy nodded. "I remember."

"Good," Kieran said and smiled. "Keep saying it, over and over, every time your hand hurts. Now, your aunt also says it's way past your bedtime, so how about you get settled into bed."

"Do I have to have more stitches?"

"No, not a single one."

Marco looked pensive. "More medicine?"

Kieran checked his watch. "Not yet. Maybe tomorrow."

"Do I have to go to school tomorrow?"

Kieran looked at Nicola and she nodded. "How about you see how you feel in the morning and then talk to your aunt about it, okay?"

The boy looked thoughtful for a moment and then nodded. "Okay."

"And keep saying the special word," Kieran said and smiled. "I promise your hand won't hurt as much."

Marco grinned a little. "Okay. Thanks, Doctor."

"And you can call me Kieran, okay? Because your aunt is a friend of mine."

"Sure thing."

Kieran turned toward Nicola. "I'll leave you to get him settled."

She stepped into the room and nodded. "Thank you for this… I don't know what I would have done otherwise…" Her words trailed off for a moment. "If you give me ten minutes, we can finish that coffee."

"Sure," he said before giving Marco the thumbs-up sign. With the promise that he'd see him soon, he headed back downstairs.

He lingered in the kitchen, ditched his jacket and hung it over the back of one of the chairs and sat at the table, looking around. Like the rest of the house, it was a modern, spacious room, with granite countertops and top-of-the-line appliances. He'd noticed an array of family pictures on the wall in the hallway when he'd arrived and quickly deduced that this was once Gino Radici's home. He'd always liked Gino. They'd played football together in high school and, as Nicola's boyfriend, they all used to hang out at JoJo's pizza parlor most afternoons. Life had been easy back when he was in high school…his parents were happy, his family was a tight unit, Liz was still alive and he'd had Nicola.

Until he blew her off.

At the time, he'd believed he was doing the right thing. Maintaining a long-distance relationship from separate colleges was never going to work. She had her ambitions, and so did he. Then, the week before graduation, when she'd brought up the idea of getting engaged he'd freaked out, suspicious that she might do something they'd regret—like deliberately get pregnant. And Kieran had no intention of being a father at eighteen. So days later, he'd ended it. Badly. He'd said he wanted to see other people. Other girls. He told her to get a life that didn't include him. Remembering how stupidly he'd behaved only amplified his guilt by a million. She'd deserved better.

When she returned to the kitchen ten minutes later, she looked tired but relieved. "He's settled…finally. And I managed to get Johnny back into bed and the video game out of his hands. Thank you," she added and sighed as she moved around the countertop. "I owe you a fresh cup of coffee."

"You don't owe me anything."

It was a pointed remark…one they both knew had little to do with the situation at hand. Their history circled in the air between them. Air that needed to be cleared once and for all.

"Kieran, I—"

"I never meant to hurt you, you know," he said quietly. "I mean, I know I did…but I was too young and too self-absorbed to fully realize what I was doing. When I did have the maturity to work out that I'd been a complete jerk, we were long gone from one another's life. But I am genuinely sorry for hurting you, Nicola."

She was still as a statue. She didn't look impressed or accepting of his apology. "Sure…whatever."

"I can leave if you—"

"I promised you more coffee," she said and turned toward the pantry. "I'll make a fresh pot. Are you hungry?"

His stomach growled and he remembered he hadn't eaten since lunch. "Yeah."

A tiny smiled lifted her mouth at the edges for a moment. "Cannoli?"

He grinned. "I still have a sweet tooth."

"I figured," she said and moved around the kitchen, making coffee and preparing the dessert on a plate.

Kieran remained where he was, watching her at her task. "How are you enjoying working at the restaurant again?"

She shrugged lightly. "It's okay. Managing the place isn't exactly my dream job…but my father needs the help, and it's kind of ingrained in my DNA to work there. I've been waiting tables at JoJo's since I was ten years old. Thankfully the place is still busy and turning a profit. I have a tourist party booked for tomorrow…twenty-four hungry mouths to feed. Friday fun, I like to call it."

"Sounds like a lot of work."

She shrugged. "Necessary. My dad has slowed down a lot in the past year."

"He had a stroke, didn't he?"

"Yes," she replied. "A few months after Gino died."

He knew she'd loved her brother. He also knew what it was like to lose a sibling. And he felt her hurt right down to his bones. But he didn't press the subject. "So, did you have your dream job in San Francisco?"

"I thought so at the time," she said. "I worked for an organic food company and managed the human resources department."

"Is that where you met your fiancé?"

Her expression narrowed, and she glanced at him. "You know about that?"

"Liam told me," he replied. "I figured Kayla told him. Why did you break up?"

She came around the counter with the coffees and the plate of cannoli, placed them on the table and sat down. "He broke it off when he realized he was still in love with his ex-wife."

He grimaced. "Ouch."

"Yes," she said and pushed the plate toward him. "It sucked. Although, probably not as much as what happened to you."

Kieran grabbed the cannoli, took a bite and then remembered how much he'd always liked Nicola's cooking. Even in high school, she'd had a flair in the kitchen. "I guess you want to know the whole story?"

She shrugged and sipped her coffee. "Like I said before, it's none of my business."

He finished the cannoli in three bites. "Okay, I won't tell you."

"Suit yourself."

He lifted up the mug, took a sip and then watched her over the rim. Her eyes had darkened, and he knew the defiant lift of her chin was a facade. She had matured into an incredibly beautiful woman, and suddenly he wasn't in any kind of hurry to finish his coffee and leave. Her eyes, the delicately arched brows, her full, pink mouth, all a riveting combination of color and lovely angles. His gaze lingered on her mouth, and he experienced a sudden tightening in his groin. He knew it was stupid, knew that thinking about Nicola as anything other than an old flame was pointless. She hadn't forgiven him. And he didn't want to get involved with anyone. But still, he wasn't quite ready to get up and end the evening.

And for the first time in forever, he actually wanted to talk.

"She left me for my best friend," he said quietly.

Her gaze met his, and she held it and tilted her head a fraction. For a second, he saw compassion in her expression, a fleeting understanding that she clearly didn't want to feel because she obviously still hated him.

"I'm sorry."

He shrugged. "Thanks."

"And the other thing?"

Discomfort pierced his chest. It was always that way. Nearly two years on, and he still felt the pain of loss and betrayal as though it were yesterday. One day, he hoped the pain would lessen, that he wouldn't wake up each morning with a hole in his heart so wide he couldn't imagine it being filled with anything or anyone. He grappled with how much to tell her and then figured there was little point in being coy or secretive about the situation. "You mean my son?"

"Yes."

He let out a long breath. "Christian. Who, it turns out, wasn't *my* son but was actually fathered by my best friend."

The sympathy in her expression returned. "How awful! You really don't have to talk about it if you don't want to."

"You can hear it from me," he said and shrugged. "Or via one of the local gossip channels."

"Okay," she said, quieter than he expected. "You can tell me about him."

Kieran's chest tightened further, and the band of pressure at his temple returned. Fatigue spread through his limbs, and he sat back in the chair. "I believed he was my son for eighteen months before my now-ex-wife admitted the truth."

Memories of that awful day bombarded his thoughts. Catching Tori and Phil together And then finding out the son he treasured was not really his child. He remembered Tori crying. Tori pleading. Tori telling him she should never have married him, that she loved someone else. Tori saying she wanted to be free of him and their marriage so she could raise Christian with the man she loved...the man who was his son's real father.

"You never suspected anything?"

He shook his head. "Phil was my colleague and best friend. Tori was my wife. I guess I trusted the wrong people."

"I'm so sorry," she said.

"Yeah," he said, aching all over. "Me, too."

Nicola's heart felt heavy in her chest. She didn't like the feeling. Didn't want to imagine that she had any feelings toward Kieran other than dislike and resentment. But...his story saddened her deeply. She'd heard it anecdotally...from Kayla and her friend Connie who worked at his family's hotel and knew everything about the O'Sullivans. So yes, she knew about his marriage ending and discovering his son was fathered by someone else. And of course she thought it was cruel and despicable. But she always managed to shrug her shoulders and wave off any feelings of sympathy or compassion for the man who had callously dumped her in front of the entire twelfth grade on the biggest day of their high school lives.

But hearing it from Kieran was different. And as much as she wanted to hang on to her resentment and rage at him in that moment, she couldn't. Particularly as he'd gone out his way to help her with Marco. Thanks to his kindness and understanding, her nephew was now safely asleep in his bed.

"So...you divorced her?"

He shrugged lightly. "We divorced each other."

"And Christian?" she asked, saying the child's name almost as a whisper.

She watched as Kieran took a sharp breath and then

sipped his coffee. "I didn't want to confuse him, you know, or make things difficult…so I had to step away."

She saw his eyes darken and experienced an odd discomfort in her chest. "That must have been hard."

"The most difficult thing I have ever done in my life."

"So, you don't have any contact now?"

"No," he replied. "I made a decision that was best for him. He needed to bond with his…with his father," he said, swallowing hard. "And Tori didn't want me interfering in her new life."

Nicola tried desperately to ignore how her heart rate increased. She didn't want to feel sympathy for him. She didn't want to feel *anything* when it came to Kieran O'Sullivan. And she didn't want to listen to his apologies, either. But she couldn't help being drawn into their conversation. She'd always been a good listener—her career in human resources had demanded it.

"So this way, only one person got hurt…is that what you're saying?"

He shrugged lightly again and picked up another cannoli. "Exactly. Everyone needed a do-over. Me included."

"And that's why you came back to Cedar River?"

"Sure," he said and took a bite. "It was time I came home anyway…with everything that was imploding here."

Nicola sipped her coffee and then looked at him over the rim of her mug. It was true, he certainly had a lot going on with his family. "Do you get along with your new brother?"

His mouth curled up at the edges. "You know me, Nic… I get along with everyone."

He was right. Kieran had a reputation for being easy-going and likable. Perfect attributes for a physician. But she wasn't fooled. "Cut the crap."

He chuckled. "Have you met Jonah?"

"A couple of times, like at Liam and Kayla's wedding. He seems very...intense."

Kieran laughed. "That's a good way to describe him. He *is* intense. And moody. And kind of unpleasant most of the time. But to be fair, he's mellowed a little over the past few months. Not that I can blame him for putting up a few walls, considering he's known about us all his life, but we didn't know about him. He still lives in Portland but visits his mother, Kathleen, regularly."

"She moved back to Cedar River," Nicola remarked and then laughed humorlessly. "We're heading back in droves."

"She wanted to spend more time with her mother and brother—you know, Kayla's grandmother and father." He shrugged. "It's become something of a confusing family tree."

She nodded a little. "And your parents are really getting a divorce?"

"So they say," he replied and sipped his coffee. "Mom can't forgive him for the infidelity, even though Dad ended his affair with Kathleen before Jonah was born."

"She's a lot younger than him, isn't she?"

"Yeah," he said and sighed heavily. "She was eighteen and in love with an older man. To be honest, I don't think my parents' marriage was ever a love match. And Dad still appears to care for Kathleen." He shrugged. "Who knows? I'm not exactly an expert on the subject of what constitutes a successful relationship."

Nicola saw weariness in his expression, and her insides took a foolish plunge. "Me neither," she admitted and managed a small smile, annoyed at herself for being so easily swayed by him, but suddenly unable to fight the feeling. "You might get married again."

"Maybe," he said quickly and drained his mug. "But I have zero interest on that score for the foreseeable future."

"Not all marriages end badly," she said and shrugged. "My parents had a happy marriage. As did Gino and his wife. And your brother and Kayla seem really happy together."

"I didn't say it wasn't possible," he remarked. "Just that I wasn't interested in the idea."

"So, you've become a cynic?"

"Exactly. Haven't you?"

Nicola shrugged again. "I'm hopeful. But next time I intend *not* falling for a man who's still in love with someone else."

"So, you want assurances?" he laughed humorlessly. "Good luck with that."

She felt her tension return. "Believing in people doesn't make me naive, Kieran. I can be as cynical as the next person. Let's face it, I've been dumped more than once and have had plenty of experience at being humiliated."

He rested his elbows on the table and stared at her. "So, I guess about now is where you swear at me in Italian?"

She got to her feet and pushed the chair back. "No, it's where I say good night."

He stood immediately and, without another word, he grabbed his jacket and made his way to the door. Nicola hurried after him and almost plowed into his back when he came to a halt outside the living room.

"Do you have a spare bulb?" he inquired and gestured into the room.

"There's no need to—"

"Just find the bulb, Nic," he said and walked into the room. "And stop being a pain in the ass."

Nicola remained in the doorway and watched as he walked across the room and flicked on a small lamp by the fireplace. "I don't have a ladder."

"No need for one," he said and pointed to the wooden chair by the window. "I'll use that."

Of course, he was nearly a foot taller than she was and would reach the ceiling easily enough. She just had to get the spare bulb from the laundry room. "Be back in a minute."

Except that her *minute* turned into about ten. There were no new bulbs in the laundry room, and she had to venture to the workshop out back and rummage through a few boxes of Gino's tools and equipment to find what she needed. She headed back inside, locking the back door and swiftly making her way through the kitchen and down the hallway. When she got to the living room, she stopped dead in her tracks.

Kieran was lying on the sofa, legs stretched out, one arm over his forehead, clearly comfortable, and obviously fast asleep.

She pulled up alongside the sofa and looked down at him. His hair was a little long, like he'd forgotten to get it cut. And the whisker growth *was* too sexy for words. His feet were crossed at the ankles, and his other hand lay across his chest. She looked at his left hand, to where his wedding band would have been, and she couldn't help wondering how long it had been since he'd taken it off. The skin was paler. So, not long, by the look of things. He must still love his ex-wife, despite what she had done to him. Love often had a way of hanging around…she'd discovered that herself in the years it took her to erase Kieran's memory from her heart.

Nicola went to tap his shoulder but then snatched her hand back. She remembered how he'd said he'd pulled a double shift at the hospital…and then he'd driven straight over to help her out with Marco. A double shift, combined with his recent move from Sioux Falls, meant he was obviously exhausted. Guilt pressed inside her chest and, instead of waking him up, she grabbed a soft chenille blanket from the love seat by the window and gently draped it over him. He didn't stir, didn't move, didn't do anything other than take a deep breath and then sigh.

As she left the room and headed upstairs, Nicola mused that, if someone had told her earlier that day that Kieran O'Sullivan would be sleeping in her house, she would have told them they were out of their mind and to go straight to hell. And she didn't want to think about how she was trying to cling onto anger and resentment because hating him made things easier. Hating him made her forget how much she had once loved him.

And hating him made her immune to falling in love with him ever again.

Chapter Three

Kieran awoke with a crick in his neck, an aching back, and two sets of curious eyes staring at him.

Marco and Johnny were both sitting on the opposite sofa clearly waiting for him to wake up. He grimaced when he spotted a ridiculously pink blanket draped over his legs and quickly swung his feet to the floor. He ran a weary hand through his hair and glanced at the clock on the wall. Seven fifty. He'd been asleep for over nine hours. And on Nicola's couch, no less!

"Did you sleep over?" Marco asked, eyes wide.

"Looks like it," he replied and stretched out his back.

"To make sure I was okay?"

"Of course," he fibbed and rubbed a hand over his face. "How are you feeling, champ?"

Marco nodded. "Okay, I guess. Aunt Nicola said I don't have to go to school today. She said I could go to JoJo's with her. But Johnny has to go to school."

The older boy scowled. "At least I've got friends at school."

"Didn't I specifically tell you boys *not* to disturb Kieran this morning?"

They all looked toward the door. Nicola stood at the

threshold, dressed in a knee-length black skirt, tucked-in white blouse and black heels. Her hair was pulled back, and she wore gold loop earrings. She held a mug in one hand, and the other hand was perched on her hip. She looked smoking hot and, as awareness curdled in his blood, Kieran tried not to stare at her—but failed.

"Breakfast is on the table," she said to the boys. "Scoot. And make sure you put the dishes in the sink when you are done."

The kids took off as though their heels were on fire, and Nicola ruffled their hair as they passed. Then, she walked into the living room and passed Kieran the mug she carried.

"Thanks," he said and inhaled the heady coffee aroma and tried not to stare at her legs. "And sorry I crashed."

She shrugged one shoulder. "Sorry I made you come here last night after pulling a double shift. I think I was a little crazy with worry and didn't think about anything else."

"Once I sat down on this cushy couch last night the fatigue hit me." He drank some coffee and grinned slightly. "Well, at least you have a comfy couch. Better than the ones that are usually in the doctors' lounges at hospitals."

Her lips curved. "Would you like breakfast? I have oatmeal on the stove."

Kieran grimaced. "No thanks."

She laughed softly. "Toast, then?"

Kieran got to his feet and straightened his jacket, figuring he must look a mess in his crumpled clothes and with five-day whisker growth. "I'm good. I need to head home to shower and change. And the patient seems chipper this morning," he said, drinking the rest of the coffee and then placing the mug on one of the lamp tables. "He said you're letting him stay home today, which is probably a good idea."

She nodded. "He can hang out at the restaurant with me."

"Didn't you say you have a large tourist group coming in today that you have to cater for? Won't he be in the way?"

Her jaw tightened. "It's too late to call a sitter. There's a lady down the street who regularly watches the boys for me, but she's not available today."

Kieran nodded, thinking it wasn't any of his business, pulled his keys from his pocket and looked at her. "Okay...well, thanks for the couch and the coffee."

"Thank you for coming over last night and helping me with Marco."

He walked past her, picking up the fragrance of her perfume, and the scent quickly hitched up his awareness a notch or two. He stopped when he reached the door and turned back to face her. Her eyes looked huge in her face, and he was overwhelmed with the sudden need to stare at her some more. She was biting her bottom lip, which she also did when she was nervous, and he wondered if she'd picked up on the weird energy that was now in the room. She was close, barely a foot away from him. Desire snaked up his spine and simmered in his blood, and he swallowed hard, thinking that he hadn't felt anything so intense for a long time.

He cleared his throat and spoke. "You know, Marco could hang out with me today. I have the next couple of days off, and I was planning on heading to the hotel this morning...my mom will be there with Liz's youngest daughter," he said, then explained how his mother looked after Tina for several hours once a week as a way to spend time with her granddaughter. "My mom loves kids. And I could drop him back at JoJo's this afternoon, once you've finished with the tourists."

She frowned. "I couldn't possibly impose on you."

"You wouldn't be," he assured her. "Marco is a great kid. Give me half an hour to get home and change, and then I'll come back."

He had no idea why, but he wanted to help her out. But she didn't look convinced. She looked like it was the last thing she wanted or needed. "I can look after my nephews by myself."

"I wasn't implying that you—"

"He'll come to work with me. Goodbye, Kieran. Thanks again."

He was being dismissed. So he left and headed home. He checked his cell on the way out, finding a message from his brother, reminding him that he'd promised to stop by the hotel on his way home from work the night before—a fact Kieran had quickly forgotten once he'd received Nicola's call for help. When he got back to his apartment, he showered, changed into jeans, a polo shirt and jacket and then drove into town. Ten minutes later, he was swinging into one the reserved spaces in the hotel parking lot.

O'Sullivan's Hotel was the best in the county. Thirty rooms, two restaurants, conference rooms and a ballroom for large functions, it had a reputation for its style, ambience and service. And his brother ran the place better than their father ever had. Liam was a hard-nosed and judgmental ass, but Kieran loved his brother dearly. As he did Sean. He was even mellowing toward Jonah the more time he spent with the man. It was hard at first, knowing his father had cheated on his mom and had a secret family in another state for nearly thirty years. But it couldn't be easy for his newfound sibling either, and he didn't plan on making things more difficult by refusing to acknowledge that he did actually have another brother.

The foyer was already busy with guests and several staff milling around the reception area assisting them, their green corporate jackets giving them a professional and upscale look. He spotted his brother by the concierge desk and headed for him. Liam looked up and waved.

"Where were you last night?" Liam asked, one eyebrow cocked. "I thought you were coming here on your way home from work. We need to talk about Mom's birthday thing."

He shrugged. "I was tied up with a favor for a friend."

Liam's eyebrows further cocked with humor. "Making *friends* already? Good for you."

His brother knew he wasn't in any kind of emotional shape to get involved with anyone…but he wasn't averse to making fun if he had the chance. Kieran shrugged indifferently, ignoring his brother's tone. "No comment."

Liam grinned. "It's a small town. You know I'll find out."

Kieran managed a wry smile. "Yes, *Godfather*," he said and shook his head. "But if you must know, I stopped by Nicola's after work," he said and then quickly explained about Marco's injury and how he had attended to him at the hospital but then glossed over Nicola's frantic phone call and didn't mention how he'd ended up sleeping on her couch.

"So," Liam mused, "you and Nicola, eh?"

"Don't be ridiculous. I need breakfast, are you coming?"

"Sure," Liam said and hooked a thumb in the direction of the restaurant. "Mom's already here, by the way. With Tina and Kayla and the baby."

Liam and Kayla's son, Jack, was three weeks old and the light of their lives. "Okay."

"Don't let Mom know you were hanging out with Nicola Radici. If you do, you know you'll get the third degree. And then Mom will start sending out wedding invitations."

Kieran spluttered. "Can't I help out an old…a former…someone I used to…"

"Keep digging," Liam mocked. "If the hole gets any bigger, you'll end up in Montana."

"Sometimes I wish I was an only child."

"Where's the fun in that?" Liam teased. "And I think it's great. It's time you came back into the land of the living. I'm tired of watching you pretend to be happy. Your fake smile makes my jaw ache."

"You know what else would make your jaw ache? My fist."

Liam laughed. "Actually, come to think of it, this is all great timing. You should join the Big Brothers program at the hospital. I've been the patron of the program for a couple of years, but I think I need to pass the baton to you. I was only talking to Nicola about it a couple of weeks back. She's been having a few problems with the younger boy… I suggested Big Brothers might be exactly what both of those kids need. And since you work at the hospital…"

Kieran's gut churned. The last thing he wanted to do was be responsible for troubled kids looking for a brother or father figure. Particularly kids linked to Nicola. Liam should have known better than to suggest such an idea to him. He wasn't anyone's father. Not now. Probably not ever again.

"I need food and coffee," he said.

Liam laughed. "Okay, let's go."

When they entered the restaurant, Kieran saw his mother and sister-in-law immediately. Kayla was stunningly beautiful, but she was also kind and clearly loved his brother dearly. And Kieran had never seen Liam happier.

His mother, Gwen, was clearly delighted to see him, and her happy expression made him smile. She liked having her chicks close by and was thrilled that Kieran had returned. He knew she worried about his brother Sean's rumored wild lifestyle in LA and would be over the moon if her youngest child decided to give up his success, money and women and return home, where she believed he belonged. But Kieran wasn't so sure of that. Sean had never been small-town. He'd always craved the action of a bigger city and had certainly carved out a successful life for himself as a music and movie producer. Kieran was different. And, for him, returning to Cedar River had been an easy decision. Staying in Sioux Falls, where everything reminded him of all he had lost, was never going to be an option.

Gwen O'Sullivan was tall and statuesque, with a silvery bob and a creaseless face that defied her sixty years. She'd been a model long ago and still carried herself as though she could grace the catwalk.

"You were missed last night," his mother said when he reached their table. "We decided you are going to be in charge of sending out the invitations."

His mother's sixtieth birthday party was going to be a big bash, with out-of-state relatives already committed to the event. *"We?"* he echoed and smiled. "How come you're on the organizing committee for your own party?"

"Well, if I leave it to you and Liam, I suspect nothing will get done," she said and raised both her brows. "Thankfully, I have Kayla and Connie to help."

Liam's wife and Liam's personal assistant. Kieran suddenly felt like apologizing for the fact that he was divorced and single and had inadvertently robbed his parent of her daughter-in-law and the grandchild she'd loved. Logically, he knew that there was no malice in his mother's words. Gwen knew what he'd been through, knew how broken he was at losing his son and his marriage. But he still experienced an acute sense of failure. From his broken relationship with Nicola to his busted marriage, he clearly sucked at commitment. He glanced toward Kayla, and his sister-in-law gave him a quick, reassuring wink, as though she knew exactly what was going on in his head.

Nothing is going on...

Watching his family, Kieran couldn't help but reflect on all he had lost. He'd loved being a father and missed Christian so much he ached inside. And he missed being a husband. And then, as always, the ache was replaced by a feeling of betrayal and rage so intense he had to take a couple of long breaths to stop the sensation taking hold.

"Everything all right?"

Liam's voice. His brother knew him better than anyone. "Yeah, fine."

"You look tired."

"I did a double shift at the hospital," he said casually.

"And then had a date with Nicola Radici."

And just like that, his hold of the situation spectacularly fell apart because two feminine sets of startled eyes immediately zoomed in on him. Kayla's eyes were as wide as saucers. His mother looked at him with a kind of delighted shock. He had to backpedal—and fast.

"It wasn't a date."

Thankfully, a couple of orders of pancakes arrived just then, but Kieran knew he wasn't about to be let off the hook so easily.

"I've always liked Nicola," Gwen said quietly. "She's a sweet girl. She's helped out on the hospital committee a few times, you know. She's so good at organizing things. I might stop by the restaurant today and see if she'd like to help me with the latest fundraiser. And the way she's taken to caring for her nephews when her brother was killed…really, such a sweet girl."

"You said that already," he muttered, feigning interest in the food his mother placed in front of him.

Liam chuckled, and Kieran scowled in his direction. Just because his brother had found his happily-ever-after with Kayla, it didn't mean that everyone else would. Kieran had believed he'd had it once…until it blew up in his face. He wasn't about to go down that road again in a hurry.

He picked up his fork. "Stop reading anything into it. She hates me, remember?"

"That's true," Kayla said and smiled. "She does."

Liam chuckled. "It's a double-edged sword, though, don't you think?"

Kieran stared at his pancakes, feeling heat rise up his chest and throat and then hit him squarely in the face. He didn't want anyone speculating about him and Nicola. Because there was no him and Nicola. Not now. Not ever again. And, when he glanced at his mother, he saw that she was still smiling, still watching him with a

curious regard that spoke volumes. He knew that look.
It was a matchmaking face.

I'm so screwed.

Tour groups were usually Nicola's favorite. They
were generally cheerful, always finished their meals
and tipped big. But today she was too tired to handle
the exuberant crowd. Her limbs felt heavy with a kind
of odd lethargy that had everything to do with the fact
she'd barely managed to get any sleep the night before.
Really, how was she supposed to sleep when Kieran
was spread out on her couch directly below her bed? If
she'd had any sense, she would have woken him up and
sent him packing. But the kindness he'd shown toward
Marco was impossible to discount. And she wasn't a
mean-spirited person—even toward the man she hated
most in the world.

Okay…so maybe that was a stretch.

It wasn't exactly hate. It was…it was anger and resentment and a whole lot of bone-deep, heart-wrenching
hurt. The way he'd ended their relationship still stung.
The pity she'd endured from her friends and the humiliation she'd experienced had been almost impossible
to bear. In the end, escaping to college in California
had been a lifeline. And, for a while, falling in love
with Carl had been a lifeline, too. After Kieran, Nicola
wasn't sure she could have those feelings again. Sure,
she'd dated in college and had had a couple of short-
term boyfriends, but no one had really touched her heart
until she met Carl. And then, once she was in love and
believed she'd finally get her fairy-tale ending, the so-
called man of her dreams simply turned out to be another man who didn't want her.

As she stacked the dishwasher with pizza trays, she

checked the time. Two o'clock. The lunch crowd had thinned out, and there was only one couple remaining at one of the booth tables. Her father was slowly shoveling the coals in the fire pit at the other end of the kitchen, while Marco did some reading in the small office off the kitchen. Josie, one of the two waitresses working that day, came through the swing doors carrying a tray of glassware.

"There's a customer out front who wants to speak to the manager," the younger woman said. "And he's kind of cute."

Nicola grinned. "What's the problem?"

Josie grinned, flashing the stud pierced in her tongue, and shrugged. "Dunno...he just asked for you."

She nodded, wiped her hands and headed through the door, expecting to find a disgruntled customer waiting for her. Instead, Kieran was standing by the counter. Suspicion coursed through her veins.

"What are you doing here?"

He gave her a grin that made her insides do a foolish flip. "Just wanted to check on the patient."

Her suspicions subsided a little. "He's in the office doing his reading."

Nicola tried not to think about how her heart was suddenly racing. After so many years, he *still* had the ability to shake her composure. Because she was as aware of him as she'd ever been.

Damn it. I'm still attracted to him.

"Is he feeling better?"

"I think so," she replied. "He hasn't complained about his hand for most of the afternoon."

"That's good," he said and looked around. "Nothing much has changed in here, has it?"

She shrugged and glanced upward, taking in the

faded bunting, dusty Chianti bottles suspended from hooks in the ceiling, and countless tiny Italian flags stuck to the walls. "Dad likes to keep things traditional."

"Does he still drive that old Impala?"

"Not since his stroke," she replied and shrugged again. "It's for sale. Interested?"

A young couple came to the counter before he could reply. They paid their check and, once she'd processed the cash through the register, she noticed that he was still watching her, one elbow perched on the edge of the counter. The customers left, and Nicola observed that they were now alone in the restaurant.

She wished he would stop smiling. Wished he would stop looking so handsome and sexy in his jeans, polo shirt and jacket. She looked for imperfections and had to struggle to find a single one. "You need a haircut."

His eyes widened, and he offered a lopsided grin as he rubbed is jaw. "I know. And a shave."

Nicola's gaze lingered on his mouth and, for one crazy second, she remembered what his lips tasted like. And since he'd been her first kiss, her first touch, her first *everything*, the memories were suddenly acute and made her knees tremble. They'd lost their virginity together. It had been nerve-racking and a little clumsy—but it had been other things too, like gentle and emotional and achingly sweet. She'd cried afterward, and he'd held her as though she was the most precious thing in his world, muttering soft words against her neck, telling her he loved her, over and over.

"Nicola? Is everything okay?"

His voice jerked her back into the present, and she shrugged a little too casually. "I can get Marco if you want to see him."

"You look tired," he remarked.

"Gee...thanks."

He grinned again and her stomach dropped. "You're still beautiful, so don't worry."

He looked as startled by his words as she did. Heat crawled up her neck, and she knew her cheeks were going to burn. He still thought she was beautiful? Realization suddenly curdled through her blood. Whatever she was feeling, he was feeling it, too. Because, after so many years, the attraction they'd once had for one another was still there.

But he also looked like he wanted to dive into a sinkhole!

"What are you *really* doing here?" she asked.

The door opened, and its bell chimed before either of them could say anything else, and then Gwen O'Sullivan entered the restaurant, carrying a cardboard box Nicola suspected was filled with donuts from the bakery down the street. She didn't seem surprised to see her son standing by the counter. In fact, she looked... well...pleased. Alarms bells pealed inside Nicola's head, but she quickly forced them back.

"Nicola," Gwen said, smiling widely. "How lovely to see you."

"Hello, Mrs. O'Sullivan." Even after so many years she still struggled to call the other woman by her first name. When she and Kieran had dated, she had spent countless hours at the big O'Sullivan house. The ranch was the most impressive in the county. "It's good to see you, too. How can I help you?"

"I bought these for your nephew," the older woman said and smiled as she placed the box on the counter. "Kieran told me about his accident, so I thought he might like a special treat."

"That's very kind of you. Thank you."

Gwen shrugged. "Well, actually, I did have something of an ulterior motive."

Nicola stilled instantly. "You did?"

"I was hoping to persuade you to volunteer for the latest hospital fund-raiser. And I'll completely understand if you can't, since you're so busy here and with your nephews."

She met Gwen's gaze and nodded. "Of course I can. Although, I'm not sure how much help I'll be."

Gwen's eyes darted quickly toward her son, and then she smiled warmly. "Oh, I'm sure you'll become invaluable."

Marco chose that moment to skip through the doors connecting to the kitchen and was clearly delighted when he spotted his favorite doctor. And even happier when Gwen announced that the donuts were for him.

"What do you need to say to Mrs. O'Sullivan?" Nicola prompted.

Her nephew nodded enthusiastically and said thank-you several times as he took the box and held it against his chest. "Do I have to share them?" Marco asked.

Nicola bit back a grin. "If you mean with Johnny, then no, you don't *have* to…but it would be the nice thing to do, don't you think?"

Marco's mouth twisted thoughtfully. "Even though he's mean to me?"

"Even then," she said and ruffled his hair a little. "Now, why don't you go and show *Nonno* your donuts and then get back to your reading?"

He nodded, said a cheerful goodbye and then skipped out of the dining area and into the kitchen. When he was out of sight, Nicola turned back toward Gwen. "Thank you for your kindness."

"He's a delightful child," Gwen said and nodded

approvingly. "You should be very proud of all you're doing for him and his brother. Losing a parent when a child is so young—it's incredibly traumatic. I know from watching my three granddaughters cope with my daughter's passing, and they still had their father. Of course, my son-in-law has now remarried, and the girls are very attached to his wife, Marissa, which was hard to watch at first…but it really has been for the best for my granddaughters. At the end of the day, if a child feels loved, then they feel safe, and Marco obviously feels like that with you."

Nicola's throat tightened and, for a moment, she felt like rushing forward and hugging the other woman for being so supportive and understanding. With only her father and her friends to offer advice, she missed having an older woman in her life, someone with experience who could offer comfort and support and tell her that she was getting some things right. In that moment, she missed her own mother so much her chest ached.

She swallowed hard and managed a smile. "Thank you. It means a lot."

Gwen nodded thoughtfully. "If you ever need anything, you can reach out anytime."

The lump in her throat intensified, and she managed a tiny nod, trying to get her thoughts away from her grief. "Uh…can I get you something? A late lunch perhaps?"

Gwen waved a hand. "Not for me, I have to get to a charity meeting at the museum," she said and sighed. "We're trying to raise more money to fund the planned extension. I'm sure Kayla has told you all about it. But since my son barely touched his breakfast and probably skipped lunch, you might just be able to persuade him to stay," she said and raised an eyebrow in Kieran's direction. "If I remember correctly, he always did have a thing for your cooking."

Within seconds, the older woman was gone, but her provocative words lingered in the air. Nicola looked toward Kieran and realized he was staring at her.

"What?" she asked sharply.

"I just love it when my mother talks about me as though I'm not in the room."

Her mouth curved. "I've always liked your mom."

"She's always liked you, too," he said and shrugged, almost as if suddenly he couldn't stand being in his own skin. "That's the problem."

"Problem?"

"Yeah," he flipped back. "A problem."

Nicola's nerves rattled. "I don't see why. Your mother and I have always been friendly."

He made an impatient sound. "Come off it, Nic. You know what I mean. She's fishing."

"Fishing?" she echoed, heat burning her cheeks as the sound of her shortened name rolled off his tongue. "For what?"

He shrugged, but his shoulders seemed incredibly tight. "For any indication that I might be ready to...you know...get back on the horse."

She frowned, working out where he was going, and not liking it one bit. "And who's the horse in the little scenario?"

"You are."

"I am?" She planted her hands on her hips as her temper flared. "I'm the horse?"

"Well, of course you're not really a—"

"A horse that you might want to *get back on*...correct?"

"I didn't mean it like—"

"Don't flatter yourself," she said hotly, glancing around to ensure Josie, Marco or her father weren't in earshot. Thankfully, they were all still in the kitchen. "Thank you for stopping by to check on Marco, but I'd like you to leave."

"You're angry."

"Damned straight!"

He took a step closer. "So, I'm guessing you've never learned how to conquer that famous temper of yours."

The blood surged in her veins. "Since my temper only comes out around you, I haven't had to worry about it."

"Look, all I'm saying is my mother seems to have developed this crazy idea that we're... That you and I are somehow... I don't know—" he said the words on an exasperated breath and ran a hand through his floppy, gorgeous hair "—reconnected."

"But we're not," she shot back quickly. "You would be the very last man on the planet that I would want to *connect* with. Next time I see your mother, I'll make sure I tell her that."

He laughed. He laughed so hard it made Nicola madder than hell.

"You sure about that?" he asked, his blue eyes glittering so brilliantly she could barely stand to look at him.

"Am I sure I'll tell your mom?" she shrugged. "Of course."

"That's not exactly what I meant."

Nicola stilled. "Do you mean about you being the last man on the planet? Sure, I meant it. And if you're offended, that's just your supersize, overinflated O'Sullivan ego talking."

He laughed again, and the sound rumbled in his chest and made her awareness of him skyrocket like a zephyr.

It's just physical attraction. She'd get over it. All she had to do was remember what a complete jerk he was, and then any stupidly lustful feelings she had aiming in his direction would spectacularly fade.

She stormed across the room and opened the door, waving one arm in a dramatic arc. "Now, take your ego, your horse analogies and every other annoying part of yourself and get the hell out of my restaurant."

He lingered for a moment, as though he had something else to say to her. But then he did leave—slowly, quietly, deliberately…and when Nicola closed the door behind him she sagged back against it, suddenly all out of energy. Because she wasn't only angry…she was hot and bothered and, even though she was loath to acknowledge the fact, her stupid hormones were raging.

By the time she'd pulled herself together, then gathered up Marco and his backpack and donuts, the assistant manager had arrived to take over from her and work through until closing. Nicola headed straight for the local elementary school to collect Johnny, and by three thirty both boys were home and out in the backyard, with Johnny shooting hoops and squabbling over donuts with Marco. The rest of the evening zoomed by, but by eight thirty the boys were finally settled and she was in kitchen, making tea and filling a bowl with pretzels. She had some bookkeeping to do for the restaurant, like selecting the following week's produce order, but she wasn't in any mood for sitting in front of a computer. Instead, she settled herself in the living room and watched television, flicking channels for a few minutes with as much interest as she could muster.

Until she heard her doorbell chime.

From her spot on the couch she noticed the sensor light was on, so she quickly got to her feet and peered through the front window, recognizing Kieran's tall, broad-shouldered frame instantly. She was through the hall in seconds and opened the door.

"What are you doing here?" she asked and held the screen back.

He held up a light bulb. "For your living room."

She stepped back and allowed him to cross the threshold, her brows up. "A bit late for a house call. Where's your car?" she asked, peering outside.

"I live two streets away. I walked."

She remembered suddenly that Kayla had mentioned he'd sublet her old apartment. So close. Too close. "I have bulbs, so you didn't have to go to this trouble."

"It's no trouble."

She held her ground and her nerve. "You're an idiot."

"Around you," he acknowledged and walked through the hall as she shut the door. "Yeah. History would say that I am an idiot." Within half a minute he had the bulb replaced and the old one was left on the mantel of the fireplace. He flicked the light on and off a couple of times and remained by the door. "Disaster averted."

Nicola stared at him, caught up in his blisteringly intense gaze. "What are you really doing here?"

He took a couple of steps toward her. There was uneasiness in his expression. And something else. Something she wasn't quite sure she had the courage to admit. Until he spoke again.

"I wanted to find out if my mother was right."

She frowned, unmoving, even when he reached her and there were barely inches of space between them. "About what?"

"About you. About me."

Nicola swallowed hard, feeling the heat radiating from his body even through the layers of clothing. She hadn't been this close to a man for so long; she hadn't seen that almost hungry look in a man's eyes since forever. And in that moment she knew that his mother *was* right. They *had* reconnected. There was no denying it, no running from it. But she knew she had to fight it.

Without another word, his hand looped around the nape of her neck, and he pulled her closer, until suddenly there was no space between them at all. Just heat and awareness and desire and memory.

And then, as though they had been transported back fifteen years, he kissed her.

Chapter Four

Kieran hadn't planned on kissing Nicola. Not ever again. But he'd forgotten how much she could make him feel. And even though he'd imagined she might push him away…she didn't.

She kissed him back.

Her lips parted, and he gently drew her tongue into his mouth, curling it around his own in a way that was shatteringly familiar. He knew her mouth. He knew the sweet taste of her lips and the erotic slide of her tongue only too well. Time hadn't diminished the memory. Time had only tucked the memory away, sending it into the shadows until this moment, and now everything re-surfaced, making the memories of her more acute than he'd believed possible. And like an old video tape set to rewind, Kieran remembered everything they had been to each other. Every recollection amplified by the next, sending his senses hurtling toward a longing he'd forgotten existed. He didn't press too close, didn't want her to feel how hotly aroused he was by her kiss.

But he wanted to haul her into his arms and kiss her like they used to kiss. Touch her like they used to touch. Possess her and feel her shudder with pleasure beneath him.

"Please," she muttered against his mouth. "Stop."

He pulled back immediately, putting space between them. Her breathing was ragged, her cheeks flushed and her lips were red. "Nic, I—"

"What do you think you're doing?" she demanded, cutting him off.

"Isn't is obvious?"

She eyes flashed angry sparks. "Well, don't do it again."

"Okay," he said and stepped back. "If that's what you want."

"It is."

Kieran took a few steps down the hallway, got to the door and then turned back to face her. "You know, Nic, it doesn't matter how much we try to deny it, we'll always have a history."

"I'd prefer to forget the past," she said and stormed past him, opening the door wide.

She might prefer it, but Kieran suspected she had as much chance of forgetting their history as he did. For three years they had been inseparable—best friends as well as young lovers. They had shared dreams and plans—and the memories were acute. Forgetting Nicola had never been an option—he'd just buried the memories deep, forging another life, blurring the lines of how much they had once meant to one another. And, yeah, now she hated him and she'd never forgiven him for the way he'd humiliated her. But there was something else, too. Kieran could feel it right through to his bones. The pull between them was still there.

"We're still attracted to one another, that much is obvious," he said bluntly and watched as her cheeks burned with color. "And it feels like unfinished business."

"We've been finished since graduation. You made that clear enough. But if you're implying that we should act on some lingering...*feelings*...well, you can forget it. I'm not interested in reconnecting, revisiting or *rewriting* history."

"Are you sure?"

Her eyes rolled. "God, you're an egotistical jerk. Yes," she insisted. "I am sure. But I do want to thank you for fixing the bulb. I appreciate your thoughtfulness."

"Just not my honesty, right?"

Her gaze sharpened. "I don't have time for...for..."

"Romance?"

She laughed. "Seriously? Is that what you think is going on?"

"I'm not really sure what's going on."

"It's sex," she said, her voice little more than a whisper, before it rose higher after she sucked in a long breath. "Obviously. And I get it...you're back in Cedar River, you're trying to readjust to being here and, despite your family living here, too, you're alone and maybe a little lonely. I understand, believe me. This town can do that to a person—you can be surrounded by people and friends and still feel alone. But now, you've discovered that *I'm* here—good old Nic—familiar and clearly struggling to work out a way to be a parent to the boys, and here *you* are—*Doctor Dreamboat*. It makes perfect sense, doesn't it?" she shot out, her face a glorious shade of pink because she was angry and passionate and clearly hating him with every fiber of her being. "We pick up where we left off, and everyone is happy—your mother, who clearly has matchmaking plans, and Marco, who thinks you hung the moon. The whole town knows how goddamned wonderful you are, I'm surprised they didn't have a ticker tape parade to celebrate your homecoming!"

There it was—her famous temper.

He'd witnessed it firsthand many times, like when he'd accidently stuck two of her fingers together with glue while they were working on a joint display project for chemistry class, or the time he'd forgotten to notice that her braces had come off three days before junior prom. She'd been a passionate girl and had matured into an even more passionate, vibrant woman. And she knocked him senseless with her beautiful hair and pink lips. She always had.

Kieran rocked back on his heels. "Good night, Nic. Sweet dreams."

He left her without another word, striding through the doorway, heading down the steps and out the front gate. A few minutes later, he was back home.

He changed into sweats, grabbed a beer from the refrigerator and then flopped onto the sofa, flipping through channels on the remote until he landed on a nature documentary. He tried to get interested in the show about animal migration but within ten minutes he was asleep.

He awoke before midnight, cursing the uncomfortable sofa—and the dreams of Nicola that kept his body achingly aroused—poured the untouched beer down the sink and then went to bed.

It was past eight the next morning when he planted his feet again on the floorboards. He got up, inhaled a bowl of cereal, drank two cups of coffee and changed into jeans, shirt and jacket. It was after nine by the time he was outside and took twenty minutes to drive to the family ranch.

Although there were still several head of cattle and a few horses running around the place, it hadn't been a working ranch for many years, not since his grandfather had gotten out of beef and into real estate. But the wide gates, endless white fencing and perfect manicured lawns and gardens made the place look like it could be on the front page of a style magazine. When they were kids, there had been a more lived-in feel around the ranch. A bike leaning against the front steps, a skateboard on the porch, Liam's old Mustang parked in the driveway. Or Liz's dogs standing point around the yard. His sister had a way of collecting animals—a pig named Frank, a mean gold rooster she called Nobby.

A familiar ache made its way deep into his bones when he thought about the sister he'd lost. Thankfully, Liz's husband ensured that their kids still had a relationship with the family, and Kieran was grateful for that. He had always liked Grady, even though their father had never considered him good enough for the only O'Sullivan daughter. Liz's death meant change for everyone involved, and Kieran knew his parents were worried they would lose their grandchildren... like they'd lost Christian.

Stepping back from his marriage and his son was the hardest thing he'd ever done. He could have fought... he could have hired a good lawyer and insisted he get some kind of regular visitation so he could maintain a relationship with the child he'd raised as his own for eighteen months. But at the end of the day, Christian *wasn't* his child. Staying in the boy's life would only add confusion and heartache to an already impossible situation. But it hurt. It hurt so much he knew he never wanted to feel that kind of despair again.

Kieran walked up through the garden and headed for the front door. His mother pulled back the screen the moment he tapped and, although she was smiling, he sensed something else was going on.

"Everything okay, Mom?" he asked as he crossed the threshold.

She nodded and ushered him down the hall. "Of course," she said, her back rigid. "So, I've got everything ready in the dining room. You might have to make two trips."

Two trips to remove all of his father's personal belongings out of the ranch house and into storage at Liam's place. With the divorce already in motion, Kieran knew there was no going back for his parents. Their marriage was over, and they were both moving on with their lives.

The dining room was littered with cardboard boxes, all taped up and labeled. His mother had been busy. Kieran glanced at her as she walked around the table, hands on hips, back straight.

"Mom, I could have packed this up. You didn't have to do it all yourself."

She half shrugged. "I needed to. Think of it as a cleansing. And it's not as though I'm attached to any of these things…they belong to your father. I simply want to start over."

Kieran understood that feeling better than most. "I get it, Mom. I just don't like the idea of you rattling around in this big house by yourself."

One silvery brow rose. "You could move in, then I wouldn't be alone."

"I'm not much company these days," he replied.

"And I want to be close to the hospital for the next few months."

She grinned. "Plus, it might ruin your reputation as Cedar River's most eligible bachelor, right?"

Heat crawled up his neck. "I don't think I—"

She laughed and touched his arm. "I'm just teasing you. Now help me with these boxes while I make some coffee. You look like you need it."

He headed down the hallway and started on several trips back to his Jeep, loading the boxes inside. On the third trip back, his mother had a mug of coffee waiting for him.

"I was talking to Liam yesterday," she remarked. "He said he'd talked to you about the Big Brothers program that is run by the hospital—as you know, I've been involved with the program for a number of years. There's a child I think would benefit from your guidance."

"Mom, I really can't commit to—"

"Nonsense," she said and waved a hand. "I know you would never turn your back on someone in need. And this child needs guidance. He lost his parents a while ago, and his—"

Kieran's suspicions soared. "Mother," he said, harder than usual. "Are you talking about one of the Radici boys?"

She shrugged. "Well, yes."

"Forget it," Kieran said quickly and grabbed another box. "I know what you're doing. You're matchmaking."

"Of course I am," she admitted.

"Well, it's got to stop."

She waved a hand. "I'm not going to stop being concerned about you. I'm not going to stop wanting to see you happy. It's been nearly two years and—"

"Twenty-one months," he corrected. "And I am happy. I'm happy to be back home."

"I know how it feels to lose a child," she said, cutting him to the core. "It feels like someone has ripped your heart out. But we have to move on. It's hard but necessary."

Kieran ignored her and swallowed the heat burning his throat, and then began walking down the hall. "I can fit a few more boxes in the Jeep."

"I'm serious about young Marco needing guidance," she said. "You've met him, so you know how troubled he is. And I think it would be good for you, too," she added. "You know, to think about someone other than yourself."

Kieran stopped midstride. He loved his mother. But sometimes she was out of line. "If you're implying that I am wallowing in self-pity these days, then you are way off base. I'm fine," he insisted. "And Marco needs his family, not some stranger who—"

"Marco needs compassion and understanding— qualities you possess by the bucketload. But," she said and waved a loose hand, "if you want to be selfish and refuse to help him, I suppose there would be someone else willing to give up their time."

Guilt hit him smack in the center of his chest. His mother should have been a shrink, he figured, since she was so good at mind games. "Okay," he said and headed off down the hall. "Sure. Whatever. I'll let you know what shifts I'm working and you can arrange something around those times. But good luck trying to get his aunt's consent. She hates me, remember."

Except she didn't kiss me back like she hated me.

Kieran shook off the memory. When he returned to the house, his mother was waiting by the door, holding out the mug again. Kieran took the cup, drank the contents quickly and passed it back to her.

"I'm sure I can get Nicola's agreement. At the end of the day, she'll want to do what's best for her nephew."

"And you think that's me?" he asked, moving back toward the dining room for another box.

"I think it will be good for you both," his mother replied.

Kieran wasn't so sure. Nicola had made her feelings abundantly clear—she wasn't interested in rekindling *anything*. And truthfully, neither was he. But his attraction to her had built momentum since that night at the hospital, and he suspected it wouldn't abate until they purged whatever was left of their connection. Which they wouldn't do. Nicola wasn't about to jump into his bed, no matter how strong their attraction. And Kieran wasn't ready for anything more.

It was a stalemate.

He knew that all he had to do was get his mother to stop interfering in his life, to get his brother to stop suggesting he get involved in the Big Brothers program, and to stay as far away from Nicola Radici as possible.

He also knew that none of that was going to happen.

It was a bad idea, Nicola thought later Wednesday afternoon. Maybe the worst of her life. Okay, not the worst. But agreeing to allow Kieran to be a Big Brother to Marco was up there with *Stupidest Choices Ever*. But Marco had been so delighted by the idea that she didn't have the heart to say no to Gwen's suggestion. Of course, she knew Kieran was talked into it by his mother. Gwen could be very persuasive.

Now she was simply waiting for him to arrive. She'd picked up Marco from school, and her nephew had quickly changed his clothes and was sitting patiently on the porch, waiting for Kieran to turn up. Johnny was upstairs doing homework, and Nicola was pacing the kitchen, thinking about how she was going to face him after her behavior the last time they'd been together.

Foolish.

Knowing how she'd willingly responded to his kiss filled her with humiliation and dread. Because she felt like such a fraud. She'd spent years avoiding any thought of him—she'd gone to college, forged a career, fallen in love, and ultimately had her heart broken—and during that time, Nicola had rarely allowed the memories of Kieran to invade her thoughts. She'd moved on. So had he. But proximity had altered everything. Now she couldn't avoid her thoughts. She couldn't avoid the way her body remembered what they had once been to one another. Because she'd never reacted to Carl the way she had to Kieran. Once upon a time, he only had to trace a fingertip along her spine and she was instantly *his*. He was her sexual Achilles' heel—the one man who could jump-start her libido with a simple look. And he'd jump-started it with a bang.

But it was just sex.

Chemistry. Alchemy. Hormones running riot.

She shook her head as if to clear it. It had been so long since she'd made love to anyone that her body was simply responding to its most basic yearnings. And being around Kieran in the past week had amplified those feelings tenfold. Sure, she *could* jump into bed with him. And she was pretty sure he wouldn't need a whole lot of encouragement. But sex without commitment had never appealed to her. Besides Kieran and Carl, she'd had one other lover, her on-again, off-again boyfriend during college. Taking random lovers wasn't in her plans, or in her nature. And she wanted to be a good role model for the boys and not confuse them by acting as though she was a single woman without responsibilities.

Sure, she liked sex as much as the next person. And she missed it. But she wasn't about to jump into the first bed that took her fancy—particularly since the other person in that bed was the one man she wanted—*needed*—to avoid.

Nicola heard Marco's excited voice and walked down the hall. Sure enough, Kieran had pulled up outside the house. He got out, locked up and moved through the front gate. In jeans, a blue sweater and a dark aviator jacket, he looked too gorgeous for words. She swallowed hard and opened the screen door, watching as Marco raced down the steps and greeted Kieran with a high five.

"You're here," her nephew said, grinning widely.

"Sure am, buddy."

When they reached the steps, Nicola spoke. "Hi."

He looked up. "Good afternoon."

The tension between them was raw and complicated and exactly what she wanted to avoid. But she plastered on her tightest smile. "It's good of you to do this."

He shrugged lightly. "No problem."

"So, we get to hang out together for a whole two hours?" Marco asked, clearly delighted by the prospect.

"We sure do," Kieran replied. "What would you like to do?"

"A video game," her nephew suggested and then held up his still-bandaged hand. "I can still press the buttons."

"Sounds good. Let's go."

Nicola opened the door and stood back as he walked

past, unwittingly inhaling the scent of his cologne, and she suppressed the sudden urge to sigh.

Get a grip, Radici. It's just cologne.

She waited until they had moved into the living room, then she closed the door, spotting Johnny standing at the top of the stairs. He looked furious, and she experienced a sharp pain in her chest. Her eldest nephew had so much anger in his heart. He wasn't as outwardly emotional or needy as his brother, but Nicola knew he was hurting. He missed Gino and Miranda so much, and most days Nicola felt like a very poor replacement for the parents he had adored. She was about to speak and offer that he join her in the kitchen, but he simply glared and then turned, heading to his room with a decisive slam of the door.

Nicola sighed, took a long breath and headed into the living room.

But she had already been usurped. They were sitting on the couch, snacking on the chips and sodas she'd placed on the coffee table, each holding a gaming console. Marco was chattering on about some game, and Kieran was listening to him with an intensity she envied. Most days, she simply covered the basics—food, clothes, school, and a reasonable bedtime. It left little time for anything else. For the most part, Nicola felt as though she was barely treading water when it came to her parenting skills.

She stood by the door and listened to the conversation, to Marco's enthusiasm and Kieran's deep voice answering his many questions. He would, she thought, make a wonderful father. Just the idea made her ache deep down in her belly. She thought about the child he'd raised as his own and then given up—it took strength and integrity to do something so selfless. Nicola wanted a child of her own and had believed she'd have her happily-ever-after with Carl, including a home and a baby. But when he had broken off their engagement, it turned her dreams to dust. Then, her brother had passed away, and she had taken guardianship of the boys, and her dreams were tucked away, forgotten alongside the life she believed she would have.

Maybe it was time she got back into circulation. She had a reliable sitter down the street, several friends in town and knew her father would watch over the boys if she needed a sitter for the evening. A night out would do her good.

Feeling suddenly better about her prospects, Nicola headed for the kitchen and began making manicotti for dinner. Once she'd popped the casserole dish into the oven, she got out her laptop and did some paperwork, including wages and ordering for the following week. She called her friend Annie and arranged to meet her and Connie for a drink and a gossip catch-up on Friday night at O'Sullivan's and then puttered around the kitchen for a while. It was nearly six o'clock when she heard Kieran's voice.

"Got a minute?"

She turned on her heels, met his gaze, wiped her hands on a tea towel and nodded. A familiar surge of awareness swept through her blood. "Sure. Video game all done?"

He lingered by the doorway. "For now. Marco's hand was aching, so he's settled on the couch reading a book."

Her heart beat faster. "Thank you for doing this. I know your mother probably pressured you into it."

"A little," he admitted and grinned. "But she's a smart woman. Tell me something, do the boys spend much time together?"

She frowned. "Not a lot. Why?"

"Marco mentioned something about Johnny blaming him for their parents' accident," he said and came into the room. "But neither boy was on the boat that day, correct?"

Nicola nodded. "That's right. They both had head colds, and Miranda didn't want them out on the water. I don't understand why Johnny would say that."

Kieran's mouth thinned. "Well, a child's perspective on things is often relative to the impact it has on their situation. In Johnny's mind, he may have blocked out the fact that he was also ill…perhaps that's why he lays the blame on his brother."

"Poor Marco," Nicola said with a heavy heart. "He's been through so much. They both have."

"That's true. But children are also surprisingly resilient. And I'm sure they both know you love them very much and will keep them safe."

Nicola's eyes suddenly burned. "I'm trying. Although sometimes I feel like a complete failure as a parent. It's not easy."

He moved around the counter. "No. And certainly not alone. I remember one time that Tori and I—"

"That's your wife?" she asked, cutting him off.

"Ex-wife," he corrected.

"Sorry," she said quickly. "I didn't mean to interrupt. I just never knew her name." Nicola met his even gaze. "Can I ask you a question?"

"Sure."

"How long ago did you take off your wedding ring?"

His eyes widened, and he glanced down at his left hand. "A few months ago."

She didn't bother to hide her surprise. "But you've been divorced for over a year, right?"

"Yes."

A heavy lump formed in her throat. "You loved her that much?"

His glittering gaze was unwavering. "No."

"I don't understand why you—"

"It was because of my…" His words trailed off for a moment. "Because of Christian. It was about staying connected. Being a part of his life even though I hadn't seen him in over twelve months. It was a way of—"

"I understand," she said quickly and came around the counter. "I mean, I get it. That's why I stayed in this house with the boys—it was a way of feeling like Gino and Miranda were still a part of things."

He shrugged loosely. "Yeah. And it also helped avoid too much unwanted…attention."

Nicola's mouth widened in a smile. "From women?"

"I wasn't ready to start anything with anyone."

Her blood heated. "And now?"

"I think you know the answer to that."

She swallowed hard, watching him, feeling the intensity between them gather momentum. And as much as her body was screaming to say *yes*, logic intervened. "Casual sex isn't the answer."

"I don't know about that," he said and shrugged lightly. "It's never been my…thing. I don't have anything by way of comparison."

It was quite the admission. "I thought you wanted to screw around in college?" she asked, remembering his words from graduation day.

Color blotched his cheeks. "I said what I had to say that day."

"You mean, so I would hate you?"

"Exactly."

"It worked," she said flatly. "I've hated you for fifteen years. Part of me still does."

"And the other part?" he asked.

Nicola shrugged. "That's the part I'm trying not to think about. I'll get over it."

"Are you sure?"

"Positive," Nicola replied. "And there's way too much history between us to start something that has no chance of going anywhere."

"On the other hand," he said and took a few steps closer, "it might be fun."

"And complicated," she added. "Who needs that?"

He laughed softly. "You're probably right. And of course, if we did anything, we'd have to stay on the down low, considering my mother is hell-bent on matchmaking at the moment."

"If," she said and rolled the word around on her tongue. "It would *just* be about sex."

He was close now, barely inches away from her. "Of course. Friends with benefits."

"Except that we're not friends," she reminded him. "We're…*frenemies*."

He chuckled. "Is that a word?"

Nicola shrugged. "I think so. It still doesn't mean I'm going to sleep with you."

"Actually, sleeping would be against the rules," he said, his voice as seductive as a caress.

"Because that sounds too much like a relationship?"

"Exactly," he replied.

Nicola turned and faced him, her hip pressed against the counter, arms crossed, her breath barely making it out of her throat. "So, this hypothetical interaction would be solely about the physical. It wouldn't be confused by…feelings?"

He nodded, looking down at her, his blue eyes glittering and intense, and desire scorched through her blood, climbing over her skin, amplifying every sense she possessed. And Nicola realized she wasn't over him. She still wanted him. And perhaps he was right. Maybe a mindless, utterly sexual encounter with him was exactly what she needed to get him out of her thoughts, once and for all. Cathartic sex. Not quite revenge, even though the lines were a little blurred. Sex to exorcise the past. Sex to banish her humiliation and heartbreak.

"Okay," she said softly.

His gaze narrowed. "'Okay'?"

She shuddered out a breath, then smiled, tugging on one side of her bottom lip with her teeth. "Let's have an affair."

Chapter Five

Kieran was still thinking about Nicola's proposal forty-eight hours later.

An affair.

Sex without strings. Sex without an emotional commitment. Sex without expectations.

It was a new concept for him. He'd had a couple of lovers during college, but met Tori just after med school and hadn't been with anyone since his divorce. But what Nicola was proposing was something else. He should have agreed immediately. It's what he wanted, to purge any lingering feelings with hot, guilt-free sex. To kiss her beautiful mouth, to lose himself in her lovely curves and feel her beneath him. Yeah…he should have agreed then and there.

Instead, he'd bailed.

And two days later he had no logical reason for his reaction.

He was back at work, tending to a busload of tourists who had all eaten bad crab cakes at a shabby diner, and trying to not think about Nicola every minute of the day.

"Dr. O'Sullivan," one of the nurses said to him as

he walked from triage toward the nurse's station, "you have a phone call. Line six."

Kieran thanked her, grabbed the telephone and pressed the button. "O'Sullivan."

"We're heading to JoJo's for dinner," Liam said without introduction. "Mom's watching Jack for a couple of hours. Six o'clock."

"Why didn't you call my cell?"

"Because you would know it was me and then wouldn't pick up."

Kieran knew his brother was right. "Can't we go to the hotel instead?"

"No," Liam replied and chuckled. "My beautiful wife wants pizza. And what she wants, she gets. We need to talk about Mom's birthday party some more. So I'll see you there."

As he ended the call, Kieran silently cursed his brother. Liam could be damned annoying at times. His brother knew him well enough to figure out he wouldn't want to spend time at JoJo's.

He spent the remainder of the afternoon in the ER and, once his shift finished at five, he headed home, showered and changed and then drove into town.

JoJo's was busy, but Kieran found his brother and family at one of the booth tables and headed directly for them. He spotted a young waitress at a table and another by the bar. The place was busy, and he looked around for Nicola as he slipped into the booth and sat down. She might be at home with the boys.

There were curly fries and bread sticks in the middle of the table and a pitcher of beer, although Kayla was drinking club soda, since she was nursing. Liam had his arm around her. Kieran watched his brother and sister-in-law together and saw the love they had for one another, the kind of love he'd once believed he had with Tori.

Now it all felt like a lie. Tori had never really loved him. She'd wanted to get married, to settle down and have a family. At the time, Kieran did, too. Looking back, he couldn't believe how blind he'd been to the truth. Because it hadn't felt like love should. It was about timing, about being a certain age and having certain expectations.

"Everything okay?" Liam asked, frowning.

Kieran shrugged. "Yeah…fine."

"It will get easier," his brother said quietly, so that only he could hear. "And one day, you will be happy again."

"Maybe," he said and drank some beer. "So, have you heard from Sean lately?"

"Not much. I know he calls Mom every couple of weeks. He's hiding so he doesn't have to deal with Mom and Dad's divorce, not to mention Jonah's existence."

Kieran grimaced. "Being angry at Jonah isn't helpful. Even if he is an obnoxious jerk most of the time."

Liam laughed. "He's growing on me, though. And, since he's my wife's cousin, he's family on both sides, so I figure I have to make more of an effort."

"Things have certainly changed a lot in the last few years," Kieran said, glancing toward Kayla and then back at his brother. "I guess change is inevitable in life."

Liam grinned. "And sometimes you just have to let life happen."

Kieran's gaze instinctively flew toward the door leading to the kitchen. And, almost as though he had conjured her up from his thoughts, Nicola appeared in the doorway, looking out-of-this-world beautiful in a long-sleeved black dress that flared over her hips and showed off her curves. Her hair was loose, and she wore bright red lipstick. And boots. Shiny black boots that reached her knees. If he hadn't been sitting down, Kieran was certain he would have dropped like a stone.

"Wowser," Liam said and whistled softly. "Looks like someone's got a hot date."

Kieran scowled at his brother, saw that Liam was grinning and then cursed the stupidity of his reaction. "She can do what she likes."

"God, you're predictable," Liam said and raised his glass in Nicola's direction.

She saw them, gestured a greeting and then met Kieran's gaze for a long and excruciating moment. He held her stare, managed to remain impervious and waited until she turned and headed through the restaurant before he took a breath.

"Why don't we order?" he suggested and grabbed a menu.

"Friday night cocktails," Kayla said and grinned. "At O'Sullivans. It's an institution. She's meeting up with friends tonight."

Liam touched her shoulder lovingly. "Do you miss being part of the single-and-mingle crew?"

"Nah," she said and smiled. "I'd much rather hang out with you guys. Besides, we promised your mother we'd be back by eight thirty. And since neither of us can bear to be away from Jack for more than a couple of hours at a time, our late nights are over for some time."

Kieran remembered that feeling. When Christian was first born, he'd never liked letting him out of his sight. And although he was genuinely happy for his brother, watching Liam with Kayla and Jack amplified his regret and feelings of loss. But with time, it would get easier. It had to.

They ordered pizza, discussed his mother's upcoming birthday party and by eight they were done. Kieran waved them off and drove down the block toward O'Sullivan's. He spotted Nicola the moment he entered the bar. She was sitting alone at the end of the bar, legs crossed, the sexy boots heightening every raunchy thought he possessed. She was staring idly into a drink that looked untouched. He walked up and sat down on the stool beside her, saying nothing. She glanced sideways, quickly recognized that it was him, and a soft smile curved her lips.

He ordered a club soda, waited for it to arrive and then spoke. "You shouldn't drink alone."

"I'm not," she said, staring ahead. "My friend Annie has just gone to the bathroom. And Connie will be here soon. Girls' night out," she said pointedly.

Kieran ignored the dismissive tone and sipped his drink. "You look incredible."

"Thank you."

He turned in the stool. "Nice boots."

"Impractical," she said and touched the top of the leather as she met his gaze. "But they were one of those things that I just *had* to have. Have you ever experienced that? You know, when there is something you simply have to have…and nothing else matters."

Yes…

Kieran stared at her, swearing she had somehow swayed toward him because she seemed close. So close that the scent she wore traveled along every sense he possessed and made his libido jump. Her red lips were tantalizing, her boots a complete turn-on, her hair so beautiful he wanted to fist a handful of it and kiss her smooth neck.

"Right now?" He smiled fractionally. "Yeah."

She met his gaze. "So, what are you doing here?"

He shrugged. "Nightcap."

Her mouth curved in a slight smile. "Liar."

Kieran didn't bother to deny it. "I thought we should talk."

"You didn't want to talk the other night," she reminded him. "You couldn't leave quick enough."

"I was in shock," he admitted.

"And now?"

"I'm wondering what you meant."

"What I meant?" she echoed. "What do you think I meant?"

"That we should sleep together."

She grinned. "I thought sleeping was out of question? Just sex, remember...no strings."

Kieran's insides did a crazy flip. Just talking to her, just being close to her scrambled his brain and sent all his good sense rushing south. But if she was offering a no-strings, no-expectations relationship, then he wasn't stupid enough to refuse. But he wasn't quite convinced she'd go through with it. The Nicola he knew wasn't a casual-sex kind of woman. "Okay."

Her eyes widened, and she sat back on the stool. "Um...great. So, when do you want to...start?"

He shrugged loosely. "You can call the shots on this one, Nic," he said and slid off the stool. He grabbed a napkin, pulled a pen from his pocket and wrote down his cell number. "Call me when you want me."

Then he left, passing her friend Annie on the way out.

I've lost my mind.

That was all Nicola could think as she stared at the bold scrawl on the paper napkin now sitting in her palm.

Her heart rate churned. *Sex without strings.* Yeah... right.

"You were right," her friend Annie said as she slid onto the stool that he'd just vacated. "He's as hot as ever."

Mortified, Nicola shook her head. "That's not what I said."

Annie's long, light brown hair swayed and she grinned. "Sure, you did...maybe not in so many words, but I'm good at reading between the lines."

Nicola took a long sip of her wine. "I'm going to sleep with him," she announced and tilted her chin. "To get him out of my system once and for all."

Annie raised a cynical eyebrow. "Do you think that will do it?"

"Yes," she replied. "It will be cathartic."

"That's not all it will be," her friend said and winked. "Just don't do something foolish like fall in love with him again."

"I won't," Nicola assured her and smiled. "I hate him too much to fall in love with him."

As the words left her mouth, Nicola tasted the lie... because she didn't hate Kieran. Sure, she'd spent the best part of fifteen rage-filled years resenting him...but she wasn't that angry, self-absorbed teenager any longer. Time had helped heal the wound. And his kindness toward Marco had made her realize that he'd changed, too. He'd always been kind...despite how cruel he'd been to her when they'd broken up.

And he was clearly a wonderful doctor and cared for his patients. He was good with kids, too. She admired those qualities. Which didn't mean she still harbored feelings for him...but it didn't mean she hated him, either.

"Have you ever had sex just for fun?" Annie asked and grinned.

"Nope," Nicola replied.

"Good luck, then. Twenty bucks says you're back in love with him within two weeks."

Nicola laughed at her friend's ridiculous suggestion. She liked Annie, but the other woman was a pure romantic.

"In love with who?" another voice said from behind them.

Connie Bedford was smiling as she greeted them. Several years younger than Nicola and Annie, Connie had worked as Liam O'Sullivan's personal assistant for five years and for J.D. prior to that and was well acquainted with all the O'Sullivans.

"One guess," Annie replied and smiled broadly.

Connie laughed and took the stool beside her. "Do you need to see a doctor?" she asked, grinning.

"No... I need to find some new friends," Nicola said and laughed.

"You'd be lost without us," Annie said and grinned. "So, when are you going to do this?"

"Do what?" Connie asked quickly.

"Sleep with you-know-who," Annie supplied and gave a wicked laugh. "Of course, we all know where that's going to lead."

"To heartbreak," Connie said, as though it was inevitable.

"Gosh," Nicola said and gave a fake grin. "You two are so good for my ego and self-confidence."

Annie tapped her arm reassuringly. "We just want to make sure you don't get hurt."

"I won't," she assured her friend. "Whatever is going

on between me and Kieran, it's complicated. I don't expect anyone to understand."

Both women nodded, and Nicola knew she was being cryptic but couldn't explain her feelings toward Kieran any other way. They were wrapped up in memory and resentment and the need to purge all her lingering humiliation. And, yes, they were clearly still attracted to one another. Perhaps because they'd had such a public breakup, their connection was inevitable. Whatever the reason, Nicola was sure the only way to rid Kieran from her thoughts once and for all was to have a whole lot of hot and wild sex with him. Then so be it. It was the price she would have to pay.

She left not long after, tired of pretending to be out having a great time. Not that she didn't enjoy the company of her friends…she did, very much so. But she wasn't in the mood to discuss her complicated love life. Not that her friends didn't have problems. Annie didn't date because she was secretly in love with her boss, and Connie didn't date because she was focused on her career. Even so, Nicola didn't want her own complicated mess to be the main topic of conversation.

Her father was watching the boys, and she picked them up at nine o'clock. Johnny was happy to leave, and Marco dozed in the back seat on the drive home. Neither of them offered any resistance when they arrived home and were sent straight to bed. Once the kids were settled, Nicola changed her clothes and tossed the boots in the closet, remembering the way Kieran had looked at her wearing the ridiculously flirtatious heels. She'd purchased the boots on a foolish whim and had never worn them before, which meant she was paying the price with some mean-looking blisters on her heels. She made green tea, placed her laptop at the kitchen table and was about to settle in for an hour of doing wages and scheduling when her cell pinged. She checked the message immediately.

I thought I'd spend some time with Marco tomorrow. And Johnny, too, if he's interested. Okay? K.

Nicola's fingers tensed around the phone. She was grateful he was committing himself to the Big Brothers idea, but she couldn't help thinking that the more time he spent with her nephews, the more it would complicate their own ridiculous relationship. *Not* that they had a relationship. They didn't have anything. Just some silly flirting and the vague intimation that they wanted to sleep together. Still, her nephew's happiness came first. And she knew Marco would flourish under Kieran's guidance. And Johnny, too, if he would agree to it. She typed a response.

Sure. They'd like that.

She waited for the familiar ping. It took a couple of minutes, and she wondered if he was having the same kind of ethical crisis that she was.

See you tomorrow. Around 10. K.

Nicola replied immediately, arranging the time before placing the phone back on the table. She spent the next hour neck-deep in scheduling and wages, but her wayward thoughts constantly strayed, thinking about seeing Kieran the following day. She turned in around midnight and woke after seven, getting little more than a few hours' sleep, since Marco had had a bad dream in the middle of the night and she had been up and down trying to console him. Once the boys were out of bed and she had made breakfast, she informed Marco that Kieran was coming over. From that moment, her excited nephew remained on the porch waiting for him. Johnny didn't seem as interested, but shrugged and said he'd think about it.

Nicola didn't do anything as obvious as hanging around on the porch but instead spent the morning busying herself with laundry and housekeeping. She was in the kitchen, making up a batch of lasagna for later, when she heard her nephew speaking excitedly, firing out questions she knew might have made anyone else run a mile. But not Kieran—he was patient and kind and listened to Marco's suggestions without so much as a frustrated sigh. And suddenly she was jealous and wishing she possessed the same quiet endurance that he did. Most days, Nicola felt as though she was hanging on by a thread, trying to figure out parenting as she went along. But Kieran was a natural, so at ease and confident. And she envied that ability.

She was wiping her hands with paper towel when she heard him speak.

"Morning, Nic."

Nicola turned and spotted him in the doorway. In jeans, a pale blue polo shirt and his aviator jacket, he looked wholly masculine. His hair was mussed, like he'd just run a hand through it, and she noticed his jaw was clean-shaven. He looked so gorgeous that her knees almost gave way when he smiled. And suddenly she was seventeen again and hopelessly in love with him. Nicola took a long breath and willed away the images that bombarded her thoughts—Kieran kissing her gently at their special spot down by the river; Kieran dancing with her behind the barn at the O'Sullivan ranch; Kieran telling her she was the love of his life after they'd made love for the first time. The memories resurfaced with a vengeance, making a mockery of every ounce of rage in her heart. Because she could handle *wanting* him. Sex was one thing. But feelings—real ones—they were harder to explain away. And she didn't want to hang on to any lingering feelings she had for Kieran—that would be plain stupid.

"Hi," she managed to say. "Where's Marco?"

"Getting a pad and pencil," he replied and moved into the kitchen. "I had an idea I wanted to run by you."

She shrugged. "Sure."

"A pond," he said and came around the counter. "Like a fishpond in the backyard. I thought it could be a good project to get Marco interested in. And help with his fear of water."

Nicola stilled. "Oh… I guess. Although I'm not sure I can afford too much—"

He waved a dismissive hand. "I'll pay for it."

"I couldn't possibly accept—"

"No point in having all the O'Sullivan money if I can't put it to good use every now and then," he said and grinned, cutting her off again. "Right?"

"I'm not a charity case," she said, her back straightening, her pride bolstering. "And I have no intention of taking—"

"Oh, for god's sake, Nic," he said impatiently, cutting her off yet again. "Stop being so damned stubborn. I want to do this. Actually, I insist," he said pointedly.

"And you always get what you want?" she shot back.

His head tilted fractionally. "Not always. Time will tell, I suppose."

Nicola wasn't even going to try to touch that one. "You're so...so..."

"I'm back!"

Marco... Nicola was grateful her nephew had bounded into the room. As he began dragging Kieran outside, her irritation turned into an inexplicable sense of gratitude. Marco was happy. And that was all that mattered. Not her old resentment, her fears or her traitorous libido. She *could* compartmentalize her feelings for Kieran and make them only about sex.

She had to.

"I think it should go right here."

Kieran raised both eyebrows and shook his head. "I don't think your aunt would appreciate a fishpond right next to the vegetable garden, do you?"

The boy's mouth twisted. "I suppose not."

Kieran looked around the yard, ignoring the twitch in his gut when he thought about Nicola. He'd been outside for about five minutes, and it still wasn't enough time to forget about the way she wound him up. She always had. Even when they'd been dating, she'd always been fiercely independent. And she hadn't shed a tear the day they broke up—instead, her notorious temper had surfaced, calling him every name she could. Not that he hadn't deserved it. He had and probably still did.

But he was suddenly tired of the animosity. He didn't want to be at war with Nicola.

He wanted her in his bed.

Kieran shook off the thought and walked around the yard. It was neat, with a swing set in one corner and a garden shed in another. And several empty garden beds that looked as though they had once thrived. The stump of an old oak tree that had been turned into a bench sat near the fence line.

"My dad made that seat for my mom," Marco said, bottom lip wobbling. "But I don't remember much about it. I miss them a lot."

"I know you do."

"But I think Johnny misses them more than me."

Kieran kept walking. "You do? Why?"

"Because he never talks about them."

The boy's logic was spot-on. It was why Kieran never spoke about Christian. Because it was too hard. Too painful. He looked up to the second story and spotted Johnny standing in the one of the windows, staring down at them and scowling before he turned away and disappeared.

"Do you think your brother might want to help out with the fishpond?"

Marco shrugged. "Dunno. He doesn't do much except play video games. He plays them even more than me."

Kieran grinned. "If it's okay with you, how about we ask him?"

Marco considered the idea, his expression suddenly serious. "I guess. As long as he's not mean to me."

"I'm sure he won't be," Kieran assured him as they reached the step by the small back porch.

Nicola was by the door, watching them, wearing a long dress that floated over her curves. Her hair was down, and her face was free of makeup. She looked young and as pretty as hell.

"So, what's the verdict?" she asked, stepping toward the edge of the porch and leaning on the balustrade. "Doable?"

"I think so," he replied. "We just have to pick the right spot."

She pointed toward an old, staggered flower bed. "Over there."

He nodded. "Sure. The ground isn't level, so it will need a bit of work, but I think it's as good a spot as any."

Her mouth curled at the edges. "Can it have a fountain?"

Kieran half smiled. "It can have anything you want."

She came down the steps. "And a sculpture?"

He expelled a breath. "Uh…sure."

The scent of her fragrance assailed his senses, and he instinctively took a step back, putting space between them. Last night, they'd talked about sex…about giving in to the desire that was clearly still between them. But today…today wasn't about that. Today was about friendship. About a connection deeper than simple sex. Not that sex was simple, either. Nothing was simple when it came to Nicola.

"And maybe it could have a light…you know, that would stay on in the evenings."

His simple fishpond idea was taking on a life of its own. "Okay… I might need to take a quick class at fishpond design school."

She laughed, and the sound hit him directly in the solar plexus. "Sorry, I'm getting carried away."

"Don't apologize," he said and passed her the notepad and pencil. "Sketch."

She shook her head. "You know I can't draw."

He did. "Just put down your ideas."

She sighed. "If you're sure…"

"Positive," he replied.

She sat down on a small garden bench by the steps and sketched for a few minutes, Marco hovering over her every stroke. They looked alike, he realized, and Kieran suddenly had a vision of Nicola with a child of her own, a girl with dancing eyes and curly dark hair. The idea hit him with the force of a freight train. Back when they'd dated, he'd been super careful about birth control, determined not to get her pregnant when they were so young. He pushed the thought away, refusing to imagine how beautiful she would look with a child growing in her belly.

His child...

"Are you okay?"

Nicola's voice, jerking him from his foolish trance. "Yes, of course."

She got up and passed him the sketch pad. "You're right," he said and grinned. "You can't draw."

Marco began to laugh, and Nicola waved her hands. "Okay, you two, stop making fun."

Kieran fought the urge to grasp her hand and pull her close because, in that moment, she was eminently kissable. His palms itched, and he quickly pushed the idea away.

"So," he said, looking at the sketch. "You want a pond, and a waterfall with a statue that looks like a tuna fish and—"

"That's a man and a woman embracing," she said indignantly and stepped closer, tracing a finger along the line of the sketch. Then she spoke softly. "See, that's the outline of the woman's..."

Kieran met her gaze, watched as her eyes widened, and her lips parted fractionally. The awareness between them ramped up a notch. And then another. He stared at her mouth, fought the overwhelming urge to kiss her. Of course, he wouldn't. Not with Marco standing close by.

"I know what it is," he said, his voice so quiet she

actually moved closer. She shivered, and he reacted instinctively, shrugging out of his jacket and draping it around her shoulders.

She protested immediately. "I couldn't possibly—"

"Keep it," he insisted, ignoring how the brisk morning air immediately etched into his bones. "So... I think I'm going to need some help with this pond."

She frowned. "What kind of help?"

He shrugged. "The professional kind."

"Meaning?"

Kieran pulled his cell from his pocket, scrolled through the saved numbers and found the one he wanted. His call was answered on the fourth ring. "Are you busy?" he asked.

"Not exactly. Why?"

"Feel like helping out your favorite brother?"

More silence. "I guess."

He rattled off Nicola's address, ended the call and then turned back to face her.

"Who was that?"

"Jonah," he supplied and saw her eyes widen. "He's in town for the weekend, visiting his mother. If you want the best job done, get the best person for the job."

She glanced toward Marco and nodded. "I think that's exactly why your mom suggested you spend time with my nephew."

"My mother is a smart woman," he said quietly. "So are you."

"With foolish inclinations," she said softly and pulled his coat tightly around her waist.

"I guess chemistry can be damned inconvenient."

"*You're* inconvenient," she said and smiled fractionally and then, when Marco wandered off for a moment, spoke again. "I've spent so long hating you...the thought of anything else is exhausting."

"The thought of us being lovers, you mean?"

He watched, fascinated, as color flooded up her neck and spotted her cheeks. Nicola was an independent, modern woman, but there were elements of her that were delightfully naive.

She shrugged a little. "I thought you'd forgotten about that."

"Forgotten?" he echoed and smiled. "We only talked about it last night. Since then it's pretty much all I can think about."

"Me, too," she admitted and sauntered off toward her nephew, hips swaying, her beautiful hair flowing in the breeze.

Suddenly he felt about seventeen years old.

And as much in love with Nicola Radici as he'd ever been.

Chapter Six

Nicola had met Jonah Rickard a few times. He was handsome and serious-looking. True, all the O'Sullivan brothers were attractive, but she'd always considered Kieran the handsomest of the group.

Love is blind...

She shuffled the thought from her head. She wasn't some giddy teenager anymore. And, sure, she suspected they were heading toward a night in bed together, but she wasn't foolish enough to think it was anything more than a kind of sexual exorcism.

Watching the brothers walk around her garden, with Marco hanging on their every word, she saw the similarities. Even though Jonah had darker hair, they shared the same walk, the same broad shoulders and many of the same mannerisms. Which was odd since they hadn't grown up together, but DNA was a strange thing. She knew Jonah was a successful architect—actually, he was an award-winning architect, one of the best in his field. She wondered what he must be thinking as his brother led him around the backyard. Nicola joined them after a while, listening as Kieran explained what she wanted.

Jonah had the sketchpad in his hand and stared at the page, turning it around a couple of times. "So, you want a statue and a waterfall?" He looked toward his brother. "In the shape of a tuna fish?"

"It's a man and a woman," Nicola said and rolled her eyes. "Embracing."

Jonah frowned. "Really?"

Kieran laughed, and she scowled instantly. "When you two have finished making fun, I'll be in the inside. I have work to do."

She left them and headed inside. She made a couple of phone calls, paid a few accounts for the restaurant and spent some time working on the menu for an upcoming event. She was closing down the laptop when there was a knock at the front door. She walked down the hall, opened up and found Connie on the other side of the screen door. She'd forgotten that her friend was dropping by with a stack of flyers promoting the upcoming rodeo. She'd promised to give them out to customers who came to JoJo's.

"Sorry I'm late," Connie said as she crossed the threshold.

"You're late?" Nicola said, checking her watch and grinning because Connie was the most organized person she knew and was never late for anything.

"I had a mishap with Mr. Jangles and the cat next door," she explained.

Mr. Jangles was one of Connie's many dogs. Her friend had a collection of strays and lived alone with them in the house that had once belonged to her grandparents. "Nothing serious I hope?"

"No," she replied and grinned. "There are a couple of cars out front. Are you having a party?"

Nicola laughed and ushered her friend through the

hall and into the kitchen. "I'm guardian to two young boys…my partying days are over. Kieran's here."

"I see," Connie said, chuckling, and she dumped the bag she was carrying on the counter. "Then I won't stay and be a third wheel."

"Fourth wheel," Nicola said and grabbed a few coffee mugs. "Jonah's here, too. The Big Brothers thing I told you about, remember?"

"I didn't realize that…that *he* was a part of that."

"*He's* not," Nicola replied, sensing that the last place Connie wanted to be was in her kitchen, since she knew her friend didn't like Jonah Rickard one iota. She didn't know much about it because Connie was an intensely private person, but it had something to do with Connie's loyalty toward the O'Sullivans and Jonah's apparent determination to hate his father, J.D. "Kieran is working on a project with Marco and needed a favor. If you're quick, you might be able to sneak away unseen."

"Good idea," she said and was just about to leave when they heard Kieran's voice.

"Hey, Connie."

When both men came through the door with Marco in their wake, the air suddenly became loaded with tension. Oh, yeah—there was so much tension between Connie and Jonah it was impossible to miss. Thankfully, it was Jonah who said he had to leave. He offered a quick goodbye to Nicola and then walked from the room. Kieran followed and, once they were out of view, Nicola hovered in the doorway, hearing their voices travel down the hallway.

"I'll talk to you later in the week," Kieran said casually.

"Sure," Jonah replied. "Oh, and next time you want a

favor, don't hide behind a story about some Big Brothers thing. Just admit that it's about a girl."

She heard the door open and close and then shuffled back behind the counter.

When Kieran returned, he was smiling. "He's such a pleasure to be around, don't you think?"

Nicola grinned. "At least he made the effort."

"He's one of those people that grows on you over time," he said, still smiling.

"Like a fungus," Connie said and then gasped. "Uh... sorry. I shouldn't have said that. I should get going. I have a load of laundry waiting for me, four pooches that need washing, and my favorite Jane Austen to read."

She was gone within a minute and, by the time Nicola returned to the kitchen after seeing her friend to the door, only Kieran remained in the room. Marco had clearly grown tired of the adult conversation and had disappeared upstairs.

"That was weird," Nicola said and took the coffee mug Kieran had poured. "Connie usually likes everyone. Your brother is obviously the exception."

"I don't think he cares whether he's liked or not. But he did agree to help out."

She nodded. "That's good of him, considering. I heard his comment, by the way. The one about why you're doing this."

"I'm doing this for Marco," he assured her. "The you-and-me thing...that's a separate issue."

"I know that. Believe me, I'm trying to compartmentalize whatever is going on here."

"How's that working out so far?" he asked and rested his rear against the counter.

She chuckled. "I'm trying to keep things real. The boys have to come first, and I don't want to get swept up in…anything that will distract me from being the best parent I can be to them. They've had enough drama in the last couple of years. And I owe that to Gino and Miranda."

"Is that why you stayed in this house?" he asked quietly.

Nicola met his gaze. "I wanted to keep things the same."

"Except that things aren't the same," he remarked.

Her back straightened, and a surge of resentment curled up her spine. "This house is filled with the memory of all they had."

"Or all they've lost."

Nicola moved around the counter and planted her hands on her hips. "Do you have an opinion about everything?"

"Pretty much."

She expelled a heavy breath. "I'm doing the best I can."

"I'm not criticizing you."

"Sure seems like it."

He reached out and cupped her cheek, trailing his thumb along her jaw. "I think you're doing an amazing job, Nic."

Her bones liquefied. Most of the time, Nicola felt like a complete failure. "Sometimes…it's so…so very…"

"I know," he said quietly, his voice suddenly like a tonic. "Being a parent can be hard work. But I think that, one day, you'll look back and realize that this will be the most important thing you have ever done."

Heat burned her eyes. "Thank you."

His gaze was blisteringly intense. "I guess you feel like you're all alone in this?"

"Mostly," she admitted and pulled away. He dropped

his hand, and she suddenly missed his warm touch. "My father's getting older, and Vince is in San Francisco… I have good friends, though, who are very supportive."

He didn't move; he simply kept their visual connection locked. "One day you'll find someone to share this with."

Nicola swallowed hard. "I'm not so sure. Taking on two kids is a big commitment for anyone. I know that Carl couldn't have done it."

His expression narrowed. "That's your ex?"

She nodded. "He wasn't ready for commitment with me, even though he'd proposed and I had said yes. The truth is, he was still hung up on his ex-wife. But we were already over by the time Gino and Miranda died. He sent me a card offering condolences, and that's the last I heard from him."

"So, he did you a favor," Kieran said quietly. "He refused to marry someone he wasn't one hundred percent in love with. Believe me, you don't want to be married to someone who isn't in love with you—no good can come of it."

"Like your ex-wife?"

He drew in a breath. "She wanted a husband…and a certain kind of life. And I made it easy for her, I guess. Tori was attractive and smart and marriage material, if that makes sense. And I was never very good at being single."

Nicola realized that they were now directly in front of one another.

"What happened to your plans for college? All that screwing around? All those girls?"

He shrugged. "Like I said before, there were fewer than you think. I only said that to—"

"To make me hate you?" she said. "Yes, I know. It worked."

"And now?" he asked.

She looked up, saw desire in his eyes and couldn't deny what they were now both thinking. Both wanting. Both needing. "Kieran... I... I want..."

"I know," he said softly, moving closer as his hand curved around her nape. "Nic," he said her name softly, almost on a whisper. "Can you find a sitter for tonight?"

"A sitter?" she whispered, mesmerized by his gentle touch, seduced by his voice because she knew exactly what he was asking. "Tonight...no. The lady down the street is away visiting her daughter in Boise until Monday. Dad goes to the home to see my grandmother every Saturday evening. And Annie is—"

"Tomorrow night?"

She could barely concentrate with the way his fingertips were caressing her skin. "Yes."

He was so close they could have easily kissed, but he didn't kiss her...he stared at her, his gaze searing, scorching her right through to her bones. She heard a noise, like footsteps on the stairs, and then quickly pulled away, putting space between them.

"I'm back!"

Marco's exuberant voice quickly defused the heat building between them, and Nicola moved back around the counter. While Kieran and her nephew sat at the table and looked over the fishpond plans, she got busy preparing an early lunch, and Marco quickly invited Kieran to join them.

"Are you sure?" Kieran asked Nicola.

She nodded vaguely. "Of course."

Nicola spent the next twenty minutes making a pile of sandwiches, pouring a pitcher of orange juice and putting on a fresh pot of coffee. When she was done, she instructed Marco to get his brother and then she set the table.

"Marco's excited about the pond," she said as she moved around the room and collected plates. "No mention of the water, either."

"No," Kieran said quietly. "He's all about the fish at the moment. I spoke to Liam about maybe taking the boys down to the jetty at his place by the river for a fishing expedition. Marco would be perfectly safe, and it might help with his fear of water. As long as you're okay with it, of course. And you'd be very welcome to come, too."

She nodded. "Yes, okay. I think that's a great idea." She sighed. "You know, you're so good with kids I almost envy you."

He smiled, and her insides tightened. "You're good with them, Nic," he assured her. "Don't ever doubt that."

The boys came into the kitchen, interrupting their conversation. Marco was beaming, but Johnny looked sullen and as though he wanted to be somewhere else. Once they were seated, she knew why.

"Can I go to my friend's house?" he asked, tearing the unwanted crust off his sandwich.

"Which friend?" she enquired.

He rattled off the name, but it was not one she recognized. "Do you have his mom's or dad's cell number?"

Johnny shook his head. "He only lives in the next street."

"No number, no visit. You know the rules."

He grunted. "Typical."

"Johnny, you know I can't allow you to visit with someone I don't know.'

There were more grunts. "I'm not hungry."

Nicola expelled an exasperated sigh, and her gaze flashed toward Kieran. He nodded slightly, as though he was agreeing with her, and it made her resolve stronger. And less alone than she'd felt in over eighteen months.

"If you can get the number, we'll discuss it. So, how about we all eat?"

"Good idea," Kieran said and grabbed a plate.

As they ate, it occurred to Nicola how absurdly normal it all seemed. Johnny grumbled his way through most of the meal, but Marco was cheerful, and Kieran entertained them with tales of his antics when he and his brothers were young. He mentioned the fishing trip idea and both boys seemed keen, though Marco was a bit more hesitant than his brother. Afterward, the kids disappeared into the yard to play, and Kieran remained to help her clean up.

"No work today?" she asked as he handed her a couple of plates.

"Back Tuesday," he explained. "Night shift until the end of the week."

She made a face. "How are you enjoying working at the hospital?"

He shrugged. "It's good. The staff are all highly competent, and the facilities are very—"

"That's not what I meant," she said and shoved him playfully, her fingertips coming into contact with rock hard forearm muscle. "I meant how are you *feeling* being there."

"Feeling?" he echoed.

"Regrets?" she asked. "Do you miss Sioux Falls? You must have had a lot of friends there and miss them."

"Like you miss San Francisco?"

"I do," she admitted and sighed. "Well, I miss some things. I miss my friends, of course. And I miss my career. And I miss Vince. I mean, he calls every week to touch base, but it's not the same as having a big brother on hand to talk things through. You've got siblings, so you know what I mean."

His mouth twitched. "Yeah, but we don't sit around talking about feelings all the time."

"But you and Liam are close?"

He nodded. "Sure. But we've had to work at it. He can be an arrogant and opinionated jerk when he wants to. Sean lives his own life in the fast lane, which is not my scene. And Jonah...well, the jury's still out on that one."

"You were close to Liz?"

She watched, fascinated as he swallowed hard. Finally, he nodded and spoke. "Yes, we were good friends as well as brother and sister."

Nicola's skin warmed with memories. "We were dating the same time she was going out with Grady. We used to say we'd be bridesmaids at each other's wedding."

He met her gaze. "But you didn't go to their wedding," he reminded her. "You were in San Francisco by then."

"We'd broken up, and the wounds were still too raw," she admitted. "But Liz understood."

"Yeah," he said and smiled. "She would. Sometimes...sometimes I miss her so much I can barely stand being in my own skin. That's the thing about loss: it never really goes away. In my job, I deal with other people's loss all the time. It's only when you get hit with it yourself that you can understand how it truly feels. Losing my sister and then my son...it gave me a different perspective. It made me want to be a better doctor," he said softly. "And a better man."

Nicola instinctively reached up and laid a hand on his shoulder. "Well, you've succeeded."

Kieran stared at her, focused solely on her upturned face and the understanding in her expression.

"Thank you," he said and covered her hand, entwining it with his own. "I don't think I've ever admitted that to anyone before. And it's probably much more than I deserve from you."

She shrugged loosely. "We all have to let go of the past at some point."

"If we want to have a future, you mean?"

"Something like that," she replied and sighed. "At the moment, I would just settle for a *now.*"

"Me, too," he said and raised her hand, pressing his mouth briefly to her knuckles. He felt her shiver, noticed the way her pupils darkened, and she bit down on her lower lip. "Since the boys are right outside and it's daytime, would it be inappropriate to say that I want to make love to you?"

Just mentioning it sent his body into overdrive. But everything about her assailed him—her skin, her hair, the scent that was uniquely hers. Pure Nicola. The one woman he had never been able to forget.

"Yes," she said and smiled. "But I want that, too. I want to get you out of my system once and for all."

It was a nice idea. But not one he was sure would work. "What if it backfires?"

"It won't," she said firmly. "I've *been* in love with you. I've had my heart broken by you. And I've been out of love with you. It's not a pattern I plan on repeating."

The raw honesty in her words rocked him to the core. "So, you think that we can successfully have a no-strings relationship, even with our history?"

"Yes," she insisted. "I think we can. I think we should. Actually, I think it's inevitable."

Kieran's libido stirred again. "So, tomorrow night?"

She nodded. "Yes."

"Uh…would you like to go to dinner first?"

"No," she replied. "It's not a date. We're not dating. We're having sex."

It sounded cut-and-dried. Almost like a business deal. He should have been jumping through hoops at the idea. But oddly, he wasn't. "Okay. My place. Seven o'clock?"

She nodded and pulled her hand free. "Sure. And thank you for spending time with Marco today. It's very kind of you."

He shrugged, faintly embarrassed. "No problem. I'll keep you posted on the pond plans. Once the work starts, I'll make sure it happens around your schedule at the restaurant."

"Thank you. I'll see you tomorrow."

"Do you need my address?"

She shook her head. "I know where you live. It used to be Kayla's apartment. So, see you then."

It was his cue to leave, and he did so quickly after saying a brief goodbye to the boys. Once he was in his car and down the street, Kieran headed into town, keen to shake off the memory of the past few hours. Knowing Liam would be working, he headed directly for the hotel and discovered his brother barking out orders by the concierge desk.

"Busy morning?" he asked, seeing his brother's frustration.

"Overbooked for the rodeo weekend," Liam said, flipping his cell into his pocket. They headed upstairs to his office. "Damned computer glitch. I now have four very unhappy customers."

"I'm sure you'll smooth it over."

"Of course," Liam replied. "I'd just rather not have to. Since Jack was born, I've spent more time at home than I have here...and it shows. And poor Connie is taking the brunt of my bad mood."

Kieran grinned. Whatever his brother's faults, honesty was at the top of the list. When they reached his office, Liam grabbed a couple of beers from the bar fridge. "Maybe you need to share the load a bit," Kieran suggested. "Find a manager to fill in when you're not here."

"The duty manager resigned last month, and I haven't replaced her."

"I'm not talking about a duty manager," Kieran said and slapped his shoulder. "I'm talking about a partner, a comanager, someone who can take the reins equally."

Liam's gaze narrowed. "Like who?"

Kieran shrugged. "I don't know...maybe you should give Connie a promotion. She's certainly earned it after being your PA for five years."

His brother frowned. "I'm not bad to work for. But you're right about Connie. Frankly, I don't know what I'd do without her."

"Be an even more bad-tempered boss."

Liam laughed. "Probably. But I'll think about your suggestion. So, how's the Big Brothers thing going?"

He shrugged again. "Okay, I guess. Marco's a good kid."

"And his aunt?"

"She's not part of the program."

Liam's mouth twisted. "Jonah said you were landscaping her garden. I wasn't sure if it was meant to be a metaphor…or whether you had developed a sudden interest in horticulture."

Kieran scowled. "News sure does travel fast. Since when have you and Jonah spent time sharing chitchat?"

"He's learning to share," Liam said, grinning. "Dissing his brother is a place to start. So, about Mom's birthday party next Saturday…are you bringing a date?"

"A date?"

"My wife is trying to finalize numbers for the catering."

Kieran drank some beer. "Then, no."

Liam dropped onto the sofa. "Coward."

"Is there a point to this question?"

"Nicola," Liam said flatly.

"Nicola's not interested in dating me," he said and wandered to the window, looking out down the street, which was unusually busy for a Saturday afternoon. "And frankly, I'm not ready to date anyone seriously."

"Bull," Liam interjected. "You've been divorced for over a year. That's long enough to—"

"You ever been divorced?" Kieran asked, harsher than usual as he turned back to face his brother. "Ever had your heart ripped out by the person who's supposed to love you the most?"

Liam looked instantly somber. "No. But I was only trying—"

"I know what you're trying to do," Kieran said, cutting him off. "And I appreciate your concern. But I have to do things in my own time. And with Nic…things are complicated."

Liam shrugged one shoulder. "You have a lot of history, so that's understandable. But sometimes history repeats itself."

Kieran looked at his brother and half smiled. "I think

getting married and having a baby has turned your brain to mush."

"Probably," Liam said agreeably. "I never imagined I could love another human being the way I love Kayla and my son."

"I understand."

"Sorry," Liam said quickly. "I didn't mean to remind you of—"

"It's okay," Kieran said and waved a hand. "Time makes things easier. And Christian is where he needs to be—with his parents. I'm grateful for the time I had with him but, at the end of the day, I'm not his father, and nothing will change that. If finding out about Jonah has shown me anything, it's that the truth is always best brought out in the open. Just think, if we'd known about our brother thirty years ago, our family would probably look very different now."

"Maybe," Liam agreed. "At the very least, we would have grown up knowing our brother."

"And perhaps he wouldn't hate J.D. as much as he does."

"Love and hate," Liam mused. "There's a fine line between them sometimes."

Kieran smiled. "You're getting philosophical in your old age."

"I'm just not prepared to waste time holding on to wasteful emotions. Or avoiding the hard stuff." Liam met his gaze. "Maybe you should try that yourself."

"I'm not ready."

"For what? A relationship? Commitment?"

"To…risk," he admitted, placing his beer on the desk. Kieran appreciated his brother's support, but Liam knew nothing about real loss. He had the woman he loved and a son that was his own. And nothing would change that. "I can't go there…not yet."

"One day, maybe?" Liam asked.

He shrugged again. "I don't know. The truth is, I haven't been involved with anyone since Tori left."

"Understandable," Liam said. "But you left Sioux Falls to start a new life, right?"

"Sure."

"So, there's nothing in your way. And Nicola is—"

"Nicola is no more interested in a serious relationship than I am. She has her nephews to think about, the restaurant, and her father is getting older. Whatever is still between us, it's just a…physical thing."

Liam grinned. "It's a place to start."

"With the potential to end badly," Kieran said, eyebrows raised.

Liam laughed. "Since when did you become such a defeatist?"

"Since my wife left me for my best friend and I found out that my son wasn't actually my son," he said, hating the way the words made him ache inside. "I don't want to hurt Nicola any more than I already have in the past. And I don't want her nephews getting too attached to me. And I don't want that for myself, either."

Liam nodded. "I get it, you know. I understand that you don't want to get close to the kids in case it doesn't work out between you and Nicola."

"It's not going to work out," he said firmly. "Nic and I are not together. We're not dating. We're just…skirting around the edges of one another."

Which meant one thing…like it or not, making love with her was out of the question.

So much for his date tomorrow night.

Chapter Seven

Nicola pulled clothes out of her dresser and realized one depressing fact—she owned not one piece of sexy underwear. And since it was Sunday afternoon, she had no chance of purchasing any unless she took the forty-minute drive to Rapid City and back. The one store in Cedar River that sold lingerie was closed Sundays. Even if it weren't, stocking up on sexy undergarments there would only set tongues wagging. She was well-known around town—as was her single status. And given that she was now guardian to a pair of young boys, hanging her reputation out to dry wasn't in the cards. Nicola didn't want her love life to be the topic of conversation for anyone.

Not that she was in any way, shape or form *in love* with Kieran O'Sullivan.

It was simply a sexual memory that had somehow been rekindled and needed to be sated. End of story. They'd have sex, and then it would be over. They were both adult enough to see that it stayed that way. Sex for pleasure. A roll in the hay. A one-night stand at best.

But as she showered and dressed in a knee-length blue dress and paler blue cardigan, Nicola felt some of her resolve slipping. She did her hair and makeup and by six was hustling the boys into the car and dropping them at her father's place for a sleepover, promising she'd be at the restaurant first thing in the morning to take them both to school. Marco was his usual curious self, but Johnny was even more sullen than usual, grunting a few responses when she said good-night, and she watched them flop onto the small sofa in the living room.

"I'll see you in the morning, Papa," she said and kissed her father's cheek. "Thank you for watching them."

Salvatore grinned. "They are my only grandchildren. I love to watch them. Now, go on your date and have a nice time," he said and winked.

"It's not a date," she insisted. "I'm just going to see a friend."

Her father shrugged and shooed her through the doorway. "Then go, or you'll be late."

She lingered by the door and then wasted time checking a few things in the restaurant before she finally made it to her car and headed down Main Street. She was a hundred yards from his driveway when she considered driving straight past and going home.

Coward...

You wanted this. You suggested it. You know it's the only way to be free of him.

Nicola pulled up outside the large Victorian and noticed that the place was lit up like a Christmas tree. She got out, locked the car and headed up the garden path. She'd been in the house several times when Kayla had occupied the second-floor apartment and had always admired the long, shuttered windows and wide veranda. There was a gazebo out back in a huge yard, and she followed the trail of lights that lit up the pathway, before entering around the side and heading upstairs. She reached the second floor a few moments later and was about to knock when the door opened, and Kieran stood in front of her. In jeans and a black shirt opened at the collar, he looked wholly masculine, and her heart skipped a beat. His hair was damp and he was clean-shaven, and she picked up the scent of some kind of citrusy cologne that wreaked havoc with her senses.

He was too damned sexy for his own good.

"Hey," he said and stepped aside to let her pass.

"I'm here," she announced and walked down the short hallway.

"So I see."

"I almost bailed," she admitted and turned on her heels when she reached the living area.

Kieran followed her footsteps. "So, why didn't you?"

She shrugged. "Because ignoring this thing between us won't make it go away."

"True," he said and moved into the kitchen area. "But if you have doubts…"

"I don't," she assured him, feeling her resolve waver but determined to go ahead with their plans. "Do you?"

"Absolutely."

"So, you've changed your mind? You don't want me?"

"Of course I want you," he said quickly. "I just don't want us to do something either of us will regret."

"I don't believe in regrets," she said flippantly. "At least, not for tonight."

"So, sex for pleasure and no strings?"

"Exactly. I don't want or expect anything from you or…*this*."

"Women generally think about sex differently than men," he remarked.

"Well, we're clearly thinking about it differently right now."

He made an impatient sound. "I just want to be clear about the boundaries here, Nic. It's easy to spout words like *no strings* or *casual sex*…but I don't want to mislead or put either of us at risk."

"There's no risk," she said. "So your conscience is safe. I have no intention of rekindling any old feelings I had for you. Not ever."

He took a moment to respond. "Okay."

Nicola stared at him, watching as he uncorked a wine bottle and poured two glasses. She saw a couple of pots on the stovetop and could smell something delicious in the air.

"Did you cook?"

"No," he replied and came around the counter to pass her a wineglass. "I ordered from the restaurant at the hotel. The chef prepared something, which I'm heating up."

"Abby did takeout?" she asked, making it clear that she knew the chef by her first name. Abby was Paristrained and had been to JoJo's several times with her young son.

"Being an O'Sullivan has its perks."

"Obviously."

He grinned. "No need to feel threatened. Nothing beats your cooking."

She met his gaze, felt the intention of his words down deep into her bones. "Stop flirting," she said and moved to the window, staring out toward the street for a moment. "We weren't doing dinner, remember? This isn't a date."

He didn't move and inch. "I know it's not a date. But since it's dinnertime, we both need to eat at some point. Don't get all worked up about it."

Her back straightened. "I'm not worked up."

His eyes darkened. "Not yet, at least."

The innuendo was not missed. "I guess that depends on how much you've learned in the last fifteen years."

He laughed, and the sexy sound reverberated down her spine. "I guess time will tell."

Nicola sipped her wine. "Such modesty."

He shrugged and moved around the couch. "Tell me why *you* almost bailed?"

"Because I've never done this before," she admitted.

"This?"

"You know, had a one-night… A casual…" Her words trailed off, and she lifted her shoulders. "I'm not much of a party girl. I've only had three lovers in my life…you, my college boyfriend and my fiancé. It's a low number for a dance card, I suppose, but casual sex has never interested me."

"Me, either," he said quietly. "But for the record, your dance card stays the same."

"Yes, I guess it does. So, since your divorce you haven't…" She didn't finish the sentence. She didn't have to. They both knew what she meant.

"No," he replied and drank some wine.

Nicola stared at him, consumed by the burning intensity in his gaze. "Why not?"

"Because I'm not wired that way," he said quietly. "I'm not like my brothers. Sean has a revolving door on his bedroom, and Liam wasn't much better before he met Kayla. But that kind of life has never interested me."

Even though she knew they weren't heading toward

any kind of future, Nicola was pleased to hear he hadn't been bed-hopping since his divorce. Even back in high school, when they'd been dating and completely in love with one another, the idea of being with anyone else was out of the question. And back then, girls clamored for the attention of all the O'Sullivan boys, particularly Kieran with his quiet, charming appeal. But Kieran had been hers...wholly and completely. Which was why his callous words on graduation day had cut so deep. Being lovers, being faithful to one another, had meant everything to her. It was as though they were in a kind of couple bubble, impervious to anyone or anything. But their breakup showed another side of him—one that had blatant disregard for the deep feelings and love they had shared for nearly three years. And it hurt. In her heart, it still did.

"How long do you think you'll stay here?" she asked, shifting her thoughts.

"I'm not sure," he replied. "My mother wants me to move back to the ranch. Since J.D. moved out, it's pretty quiet out there."

"Are you tempted?"

"A little. I'm happier staying close to the hospital for the moment. But it was great growing up on the ranch. There's something soothing about wide-open spaces."

"I wouldn't know," she mused. "I spent my child-hood living above the restaurant and then sharing a dorm room at college before I moved into my apartment in San Francisco. But I remember spending time at the ranch when we were young. I remember the loft in the barn."

"Me, too," he said. "We had some fun times in that loft. But the ranch is too big for a just a couple of people. It needs a family in it. Liam's not interested in living there, since he and Kayla have that big house down by the river. I don't know, maybe she should sell the place and start afresh."

Nicola sighed. "She and your dad were married a long time—it would be hard to let go completely."

"For sure, but divorce changes everything. And Dad is spending time working on his relationship with Jonah—which I think he should do—but that means he's not quite as alone as my mom. The whole situation is confusing and complex."

"Like most families," she added. "Spend a day in mine. My father is sad all the time, my brother won't come back to Cedar River because he blames himself for Gino's death and I'm trying to be the glue that keeps it all together."

"You think Vince blames himself?"

She nodded. "Vince insisted Gino and Miranda go sailing, even though she wanted to stay at the apartment because both the boys weren't feeling well. He said the boys would be fine. And then Gino and Miranda died. Instant self-blame."

"That's got to be tough," Kieran said and moved into the kitchen. "I mean, it was an accident."

"I know," she replied. "But loving someone takes all the logic out of things, doesn't it?"

He half smiled. "Yeah, it sure does."

Nicola felt the edge to his words and thought about all he had lost—his wife, his son and his sister all in the space of a few short years. "Do you miss being married?"

"Yes," he replied and smiled. "I was good at it."

"I'm sure you were. Maybe you'll get married again one day."

He shrugged a little. "Maybe. But next time I'll

choose someone who is actually in love with me and doesn't prefer my best friend."

She shuddered. "I can't imagine how hard that was. I mean, Carl and I broke up because he still had feelings for his ex-wife...but he was honest about it once we'd become engaged and once he knew he still had those feelings. But the idea of lying to someone so blatantly like she did to you...it's difficult to comprehend."

"I don't think it was intentional," he said quietly. "I don't think either of them deliberately set out to fall in love and have an affair. Phil was living with someone... Tori and I were married...and we were all friends. Nothing seemed off-kilter until the day I caught them in bed together."

Nicola gasped. "You found them together. Wow, how awful."

He laughed humorlessly. "It was certainly a shock."

"Did she admit to the other thing straightaway?"

"You mean that my son wasn't actually my son?" he queried and pulled a couple of plates from the cupboard. "Not long after. I think by then she was relieved that it was out in the open. So I moved out, and she moved on."

Nicola walked toward the counter and placed her glass down, meeting his gaze steadily. "How do you..." She stopped, her words trailing off.

"How do I what?" he queried.

She took a steadying breath. "How do you trust anyone again after that?"

He shook his head. "Honestly, I have no idea. A part of me wonders, if I ever do get seriously involved with someone again, how I won't question everything. But I don't want to be that person, Nic. I don't want to be suspicious and paranoid and uncertain because that's no way to live a life. The truth is, I'm not sure if I'll ever have the courage to get married again or have kids. I don't know if I'll always be thinking *Is she being faithful?* or *Is this child really mine?* It's too early, I guess. Too raw."

Nicola swallowed the tightness in her throat. "I'm sorry that happened to you."

"Yeah, me, too."

In that moment, her earlier reservations slipped away. Because there were just the two of them in the room, two slightly broken people who had somehow found a way back to one another, even if it was simply for a few hours.

She met his gaze head on and stepped back. "Can we skip dinner?"

He stilled. "If that's what you want."

Nicola nodded and moved back, heading around the sofa. She took a breath, let the air fill her lungs and flow through her veins and then spoke. "Come here."

He moved around the kitchen counter and stood in front of her, looking all serious and gorgeous. "Okay, I'm here."

She raised one eyebrow. "Sit down."

He did as she requested, settling onto the sofa, arms draped across the back. "Okay, I'm sitting."

Nicola moved in front of him, her legs in front of his knees. She took a breath, galvanized her back bone and then smiled. He returned the gesture, his eyes darkening, his gaze unwavering. She moved toward the sofa and straddled his lap, holding on to his shoulders, feeling the muscles bunch and tense beneath her palm and fingertips. There was something intensely erotic about the moment, as though they were the only two people on the planet. And to his credit, he didn't move. He didn't make an instant and gratuitous grab for her. That wasn't his style. He simply stared deep into her eyes, maintaining a visual contact that was so intense it burned her right through to her bones. She pressed closer, feeling him harden against her, feeling his body in a way she hadn't for fifteen years. He'd changed some, filled out, gotten broader in the shoulders and added muscle to his bones. He was no longer a boy. She was no longer a girl. He was a man; she was a woman. And they were both experienced in life and love and loss.

Nicola traced her hands along his shoulders and reached his neck, gently threading her fingers through his hair. Long ago, his hair had been longer, but it was still silky and sexy between her fingers. She touched his jaw with the back of her hand and realized how labored his breathing was, as though every ounce of air was a battle.

"Are you okay?" she asked.

He smiled fractionally. "I'm fine."

"I'm just getting reacquainted."

His mouth twisted sexily. "I know exactly what you're doing, Nic."

Heat pitched in her belly, and she pressed closer, waiting for his arms to come around her and for his hands to latch on to her hips. But they didn't. He hadn't moved. Except for the hard length of him pressing directly against her through his jeans and his deep breathing, he hadn't so much as twitched a muscle.

"Are you playing hard to get?"

He chuckled deeply. "I told you the other night— you call the shots."

Her blood surged, pooling directly between her thighs, and she instinctively pressed closer. "Which means what, exactly?"

"Which means—" he said, his gaze traveling down

her neck and over her breasts for a moment before he reached her eyes again "—ask me."

"Ask you?"

"Ask me to kiss you," he replied, the tiny pulse in his cheek throbbing madly. "Ask me to make love to you. Ask me to be inside you."

Nicola's libido surged, and she sucked in a sharp breath. "Kiss me?"

He draped a hand around her neck, anchoring her head, drawing her closer, and then his mouth was on hers. Not gently. Not softly. But exactly what she wanted, their lips together, their tongues together, fused by a need that was both thrilling and terrifying.

Then he pulled back abruptly, leaving her panting and wanting more. "And what else?" he demanded, skimming his hands down her sides and holding her hips. "What else do you want?"

She pushed closer, feeling him hard, and she reached down between them, pressed her palm against him through the rough denim. "Make love to me. I want to feel you inside me."

He groaned, kissing her again, his hands grinding her hips seductively, and then he pushed her dress up her thighs. Nicola met his tongue with her own, and they did a sexy dance in her mouth as his hand moved between her legs. She almost bucked off the couch when his fingers slipped beneath her panties, and he found her moist and ready for him. He touched her intimately, finding a rhythm within seconds, and she climaxed almost immediately, gasping his name as pleasure rocked through her, wave after wave pulsing across her skin, through her blood and deep down into the far reaches of her soul. Then his mouth was on her throat, his free hand gently kneading her breast before he effortlessly started undoing the buttons on her sweater. She ground her hips against him, feeling his hardness, wanting him inside her with such intensity she could scarcely breathe.

"You're so beautiful, Nic," he whispered against her throat, tracing his mouth around to the sensitive spot behind her ear as he plunged one hand into her hair, twisting the locks gently, before claiming her lips again.

Nicola grappled clumsily with the top button on his jeans and had just slipped it open when she heard a sound. A ringing. A cell phone. She had some faraway thought that it was Kieran's cell because he was probably on call for the hospital. But after a moment, she recognized the ring and groaned heavily.

"Is that you or me?" he muttered against her lips.

"Me," she said, agonized as she pulled back. "I have to get it. My father is watching the boys, and I—"

"Then, get it," he said softly and grabbed her hips, pushing her back until she was standing on unsteady feet.

Nicola straightened her dress and took a few wobbly steps. She grabbed her tote from the spot she'd left it and rummaged clumsily for her cell. It was still ringing, and she answered it in a breathless rush. Moments later, she ended the call and turned to face Kieran. He was now standing, his clothes back in perfect position.

"I have to go," she said, heat pricking the back of her eyes. "I'm sorry."

He frowned, stepping closer. "What's wrong?"

She shook her head, her thoughts completely jumbled. "That was Hank Culhane, the police chief," she explained and threw the tote over one shoulder. "Johnny's been arrested."

* * *

Breaking and entering. Theft. Willful damage. The list of offenses from Johnny's crime spree was long. Kieran knew that Nicola was barely hanging on by a thread as the police officer explained how her nephew had snuck out of the apartment after bedtime, had met up with a friend and broken into the bakery down the street. They had shattered two windows, damaged the cash register and sprayed paint in the kitchen. The fact that he hadn't acted alone and had the help of a friend was of little consequence. This was *her* nephew they were talking about.

She was hurting. She was angry. She was clearly unsure what to say or do. He also suspected she wasn't sure if she wanted him around witnessing the whole event. But he wasn't going anywhere. She needed someone to lean on, and he wasn't about to bail.

He stayed with her while she called her father and explained what had happened, and then spent several minutes speaking in Italian to her clearly distressed parent.

"Is Salvatore okay?" Kieran asked when she ended the call.

"Stressed out," she replied. "Like me. He had no idea Johnny had snuck out. Thankfully Marco is still sound asleep. Poor Papa...he'll be blaming himself for this."

"It's not your dad's fault," Kieran assured her. "Or yours."

"It sure feels like it," she admitted. "Maybe, but it's not."

"I can't believe he'd do this," she said, when they were alone and the police officer had gone to collect her nephew from an adjoining office. "What was he thinking?"

Kieran touched her hand. "He's acting out his grief, Nic. It's not so hard to understand."

"But stealing? And the damage. God, how am I supposed to pay for this?"

He squeezed her fingers. "The place is insured."

"How do you know that?"

"Because the baker, Mr. Phelps, is a reasonable man." He smiled. "And my family owns the building, so I know the landlords are fair. You can stop stressing."

She rolled her beautiful eyes. "Great… Liam's gonna have a fit."

"Liam won't do any such thing," he assured her. "I can handle my brother. Let's just get Johnny home and leave the other stuff for another day."

"Does that include you and me?"

"Yes," he replied.

"Doesn't my crazy life make you want to run a mile?"

Kieran didn't want to run. He wanted to help her. "Not at all."

She was about to respond when the door opened and the police officer ushered Johnny into the room. The boy had his head bent, his eyes downcast, his feet barely managing a shuffle across the linoleum.

"Johnny," she said and sighed. "How could you?"

The child shrugged. "What do you care?"

Kieran saw her tense, and she got to her feet. "I care," she insisted. "You're my nephew. Of course I care."

"You care about Marco," he said and looked up, tears in his eyes. "No one cares about me. My mom and dad are dead."

"I know they are. And I know you miss them. I miss them, too. But you have me, and Marco and *Nonno*, and we all care about you."

He shrugged and tugged his hoodie over his head. "Can we go home now?"

Kieran looked toward the police officer, and he nodded slightly, then looked at Nicola. "I'll get Hank to give you a call tomorrow. Bill Phelps might press charges and want damages paid for but, considering Johnny's age and how he hasn't ever done anything like this before, I'm sure we can sort something out."

They both thanked the officer and, once they were outside, Kieran said he'd follow her to the restaurant to collect Marco and then see them safely home.

"You don't have to do that," she said and shuffled Johnny into her car.

"I know I don't have to," he said and opened her door. "But I want to. Let's go."

They pulled into the driveway about twenty minutes later. Salvatore couldn't believe that Johnny had snuck out, and a confused Marco was happy to be home and to see Kieran. He had no idea what had transpired with his older brother, which was a good thing. It took another twenty minutes to get him to go to bed and, while Nicola did that, Kieran sat at the kitchen table with Johnny.

"I guess I'm grounded now?" the boy said and pulled back the hoodie.

"Probably," Kieran replied.

Johnny looked up and frowned. "Are you gonna marry my aunt?"

Kieran almost fell off the chair. "Uh…no, certainly not."

"Why not?" Johnny shot back. "I thought you liked her."

Kieran chose his words carefully. "Of course I like her. We're friends. But that's all."

"Then how is she supposed to get a boyfriend if

you're hanging around?" he asked, grunting the question out.

Kieran had to fumble for a reply. "You want your aunt to have a boyfriend?"

"Sure," he muttered. "Then she might get married. And we'd be a real family again."

Kieran relaxed in the chair. Johnny's childish logic made perfect sense for a ten-year-old. He wanted a family like the one he used to have. He wanted things to return to how they had once been.

Stand in line, kid.

"I'm sure your aunt will get married one day, if that's what she wants," Kieran said quietly.

Johnny shrugged angrily. "Not if you're here."

"So, you want me to stop coming around?"

Johnny made another grunting sound and twisted his hands together. "I didn't say that."

"So, it's okay if I come here to see you and Marco?"

Johnny shrugged again. "I guess. I mean, you're kinda cool."

Kieran smiled. "Thanks. I think you're cool, too."

Johnny twisted his hands together. "Would it be okay if I started hanging out with you and Marco?"

"Sure," Kieran replied.

"And you could come and see Aunt Nicola, too…if that's what you want. I mean, I think she'd like that."

"And you'd be okay with that?" Kieran asked quietly.

Johnny nodded. "Yeah…if you like her."

"I like her," Kieran said. "We're friends."

Johnny met his gaze, chewing on his lower lip. "I just want things to be different. I dunno… I want Aunt Nicola to be happy. And how can she be happy if she's gotta look after me and Marco all the time? And, if she's not happy, then maybe she won't want to look after us forever. And *Nonno*'s really old, so he *can't* look after us forever. But if Aunt Nicola got married, she'd have a husband, and we could live in his house, and she'd be happy all the time and wouldn't care if me and Marco were here, too."

The hurt in Johnny's voice could not be missed, and Kieran's insides contracted. "So, you don't want to live in this house?"

He shrugged again. "I don't like it here anymore."

Kieran's attention was diverted toward the door, and he spotted Nicola hovering at the threshold. Her eyes glistened, and seeing her pain made his chest ache. He fought the urge to rush across the room and hold her close, to reassure her that everything would be okay. But he didn't.

She came into the room and walked around the table, stopping behind Johnny. She placed her hands on his narrow shoulders, squeezed him gently and kissed the top of his head. "How about you head off to bed, okay? We'll talk in the morning." Leaning over, she wrapped him in her arms and hugged him tightly. "I do love you, kiddo," she whispered. "No matter what."

Johnny muttered a swift good-night and left the room quietly, wiping tears from his face as he walked away. Nicola dropped into the chair the boy had vacated, propped her elbows on the table and let out an agonizing sigh.

"I suck at being a parent."

Kieran smiled gently. "No, you don't. It's been a hard day, certainly. But not every day will be hard. Some days will be good. Other days will be great. Accept that you're going to make mistakes."

"Like staying in this house?" she said and shuddered. "I overheard some of what Johnny was saying. I guess

I thought I was doing the right thing. I thought…it was best for the boys. But all I did was try and make it easier for myself."

Kieran reached across the table and grasped her hand, entwining their fingers intimately. "It's time to have some compassion for yourself, Nic. You did what you thought was right. At the end of the day, that's all you can do."

She inhaled deeply and offered a tight smile. "You're good at this, you know."

"I've had some practice," he said and grinned. "Occupational hazard."

Her fingers tightened around his. "I'm glad you're here. I needed a friend tonight. Even one who is getting in the way of me finding a husband."

Kieran's eyes widened. "You heard Johnny say *that*?"

"I heard. He wants a family like he used to have. So, I guess I should start looking for a boyfriend," she said wryly. "Any ideas?"

He laughed softly. "Don't ask me to play Cupid. That's my mother's department."

"Maybe she could help?" she suggested and then looked in the direction of the doorway for a moment, before her voice dropped in volume. "But before she does, I think we need to finish what we started."

Kieran's stomach took a dive. "Are you sure?"

"Positive," she replied and rubbed her thumb along his palm. "Only, next time, we'll try and make it to the bedroom."

"Or not," he said and released her as he got to his feet and moved around the table. "And now I'm going to salvage what's left of my good sense and get out of here so you can get some rest. Good night, Nic."

He kissed her soundly, lingering a little to taste her

sweet mouth before he straightened and left. But he was still thinking about her hours later. And suspected it would take more than one night to get Nicola from his thoughts. He'd had fifteen years, and it hadn't worked.

Because she wasn't only in his thoughts. She was in his heart.

And he wasn't sure he would ever get her out.

Chapter Eight

Nicola had a hard week. She spent as much time with Johnny as she could, as well as working at the restaurant and making peace with Mr. Phelps. She found herself in the clear, with nothing owed and all charges against Johnny dropped. Of course, she knew why.

Kieran.

A veritable knight in shining armor.

He'd stopped by the house several times during the week. Once with Jonah on the phone to go over plans for the fishpond, and once to hang out with the boys—both of them this time—to watch a movie and help make a cart for Johnny's fishing tackle. And then again to bring takeout from O'Sullivan's because she'd had a particularly long day at the restaurant and both boys had been misbehaving one afternoon. The boys had made plans to go fishing, and Marco's enthusiasm was beginning to outweigh his nerves, or so it appeared. Her gratitude toward Kieran was growing daily. He had patience and showed genuine care for her nephews. And with every visit, every conversation, she felt just a little less alone. She knew he was working and fitting the visits in between his shifts at the hospital, and she appreciated his attention to both Marco and Johnny. The problem was she was getting used to him stopping by, and that in itself presented a problem. Because they were friends.

That's all…

He'd said as much to Johnny the night they'd collected him from the police station. The night they'd almost made love. The night she'd experienced true passion for the first time in forever and had responded like a woman who was hopelessly and completely in love. Except that she wasn't. She couldn't be. She'd stopped being in love with Kieran fifteen years ago. To go back to that…it was crazy thinking.

She'd made plans to sleep with him and then forget all about him.

Simple.

Not…

Because a woman could never forget the first man she'd loved.

"Everything okay, Nicola?"

She looked up from her task of peeling cling wrap off an assortment of dishes and smiled. Gwen O'Sullivan was on the other side of the counter, watching her, her brows angled curiously.

"Of course," she said and kept working. "And thank you for the invitation today. The boys are delighted to be here."

The invitation to attend Gwen's birthday celebration had come from Kieran—via his mother, she suspected—and, once the boys knew it was being held at the ranch and that there would be pony rides for the kids and an assortment of other activities, they had insisted on going. And, since Nicola was keen to see them happy, she hadn't been able to refuse the invitation.

"I'm delighted to have you here," Gwen said and

smiled. "Not that I'm keen on turning sixty, but I'm loving the fact that my children and grandchildren are here to celebrate it with me. And friends—old and new. And some, like yourself, a little of both."

Nicola smiled warmly. She genuinely liked Gwen, and being around the older woman made her miss her own mother so much she ached inside.

And the ranch held so many special memories for her. When she was young, she'd spent countless hours in the kitchen with Gwen, going over recipes, talking about fashion and music and favorite television shows. The big house had always been full of people and lots of love and laughter.

It seemed quieter now, somehow, even though there were close to fifty people beneath the tent set out on the back lawn. Kayla was in the kitchen, as was Connie, and Nicola was pleased to have her friend close on hand. Even if Connie seemed unusually tense for most of the afternoon, something she suspected had to do with the fact that Jonah Rickard had made an unexpected visit. He spent most of the time talking to Liam and Kieran and left after dropping a wrapped box onto the gift table. Nicola admired his gumption, since he had every reason to stay away. But he appeared to have genuine respect for Gwen, and she knew it was reciprocated.

Nicola was surprised to see that Sean had also arrived, since he rarely showed his face in town. Liz's daughters were also there with their father, Grady, and his wife, Marissa, who Nicola remembered from high school. As she mingled through the crowd that afternoon, she realized how small a town Cedar River was. Even though she'd been gone for over a decade and only back for a year, she knew almost everyone.

"Okay," Gwen said and ushered them all from the

kitchen. "We'll let the caterers do the rest. I want you all out in the tent and having a good time. Off you go."

A buffet lunch was served about fifteen minutes later, and Nicola was returning to the table alone when Kieran sidled up beside her. "Plan on saving me a seat?" he asked.

She shrugged and compared her modest plate with his overflowing one. "Only if you let me have a buffalo wing," she said and sat down.

He slid in beside her and dropped the chicken onto her plate. "You owe me."

"Don't I know it," she said and smiled, remembering how she'd fallen apart in his arms at his apartment while he'd gone without release. "I'll make it up to you."

"When?" he teased.

"Tonight?"

He shook his head. "Can't. Working." He checked his watch. "In fact, I'm out of here in about forty-five minutes."

"Oh…okay."

He gave her a heated look. "If you get a sitter Tuesday night, we could finish what we started."

She swallowed hard, fighting the nerves that suddenly filled her blood. "Sure."

"Unless you've changed your mind?"

"Of course not," she shot back and smiled extra sweetly. "I want to get you out of my system once and for all."

His gaze darkened. "It's a date," he said and then shrugged. "I know, I know…it's not a date. We don't date."

"That's right," she insisted.

She spotted Liam at the next table as he smiled and winked, like he knew exactly what was going on. She glared at Kieran, then jabbed him in the ribs with her elbow. "Did you tell your brother what's going on between us?"

"Of course not," he replied quietly. "I'm not indiscreet."

"He looks like he knows."

Kieran looked up, glared at his grinning brother for a moment and then focused his attention back on her. "He's just being a pain in the ass."

"Why?"

"Because he can be," he replied. "Ignore him."

"And I thought my family was weird."

He chuckled. "Gino used to antagonize you all the time. So did Vince. That's what families do. It's one of the reasons why I love mine so much."

Her heart contracted. "That's nice. You really are a soppy sentimentalist."

"Is that a compliment?"

"Definitely," she said, smiling. "You're still the sweetest O'Sullivan."

"Sweet?" he grimaced. "Gee…thanks."

"You know what I mean," she said and waved a hand. "It's like, if you and your brothers were lined up, Sean's the O'Sullivan who women avoid because he's the bad boy, Liam's the one who's pined over, Jonah's the moody, tortured one…and then you…the one the girls want to marry. Honest, reliable, faithful…sweet."

"That makes me sound as boring as a shoe."

Heat scorched her cheeks. She wanted to backpedal. She wanted to stop talking to Kieran about marriage and all his endearing qualities. Because the more she talked, the more chance he had of figuring out that she was on the brink of being halfway to falling in love with him again.

Because he *was* the kind of man a girl wanted to marry. The fact he'd told Johnny he would *certainly* not be marrying her pained more than she'd believed possible. Because Carl hadn't wanted to marry her, either. And the notion that she was not marriage material hurt right through to her bones.

"You're not," she said, unable to stop the words from pouring out. "You're rock-solid. The guy who gives women faith in men, even when they've had their heart broken."

His gaze didn't waver. "Now who's being sweet, huh?"

"I guess we both have a lot to offer," she said softly and shrugged. "It's just a matter of finding the right person to share it with."

"Yeah," he said and rested a hand on her thigh beneath the table. "There's that."

"I don't have any illusions about us, Kieran," she said, feeling her desire for him spike. "Once we get one another out of our systems, we can move on. It's what I want. What I need. What happened with Johnny last weekend made me realize I need to think about people other than myself. And once we're done, I can do that."

"Sure," he said and quickly moved his hand. "Whatever. I'll see you soon."

He pushed the plate aside, got to his feet and left the table. Connie, who was on the other side of the table, moved around and took his spot. "What was that all about?" she asked, her voice little more than a whisper.

Nicola sighed. "Just Kieran and I being *Kieran and I*. History makes it complicated."

Connie frowned. "Be careful, okay?"

"I will be," she promised her friend. "Kieran's no more interested in anything serious than I am." She raised a brow. "Anyway, I'd much rather talk about you and Jonah."

Connie's cheek spotted with color. "Don't ask."

"You like him?"

"Not one bit," her friend said dismissively. "He's the most arrogant, self-centered jerk I've ever met."

"Love and hate," Nicola said and grinned. "You never did really tell me what happened all those months ago."

Connie shrugged. "I guess we all have our own history."

Nicola knew much about her friend's past, but it was never spoken of. Some things were best left unsaid. She patted Connie's arm and finished her meal, conscious of Kieran at the other end of the tent. He left about half an hour later, without speaking to her again, although she did observe him saying goodbye to the boys who were still bounding around on the bouncy castle. She had a chance to speak to Liam before she left, thanking him for running interference with the bakery owner.

"Not a problem," he said, his arms cradling his newborn son. "But I didn't really do anything. Kieran did the sorting. You know how he is."

Yes, she did. "He likes to help people," she said, heat rising up her neck.

"He likes helping *you*," Liam remarked. "And he's genuinely fond of your nephews. Don't mess him up, okay?" Liam said more seriously. "He's been through enough these past couple of years."

Nicola's eyes widened. "I don't know what you—"

"I know the two of you are skirting around the edges of something," he replied. "His words, not mine. But it's clear that something's going on. Just make sure it's for the right reasons." He looked toward the jumping castle and then glanced at his own son. "Kids have a way of changing things."

"I know that," Nicola said, straightening her shoulders. "But for the record, your brother isn't in any danger of being messed with."

"You've always been his Kryptonite, Nicola...that'll never change."

He walked off before she could reply. But that was just as well. The truth was she had no response to such a revelation.

Kieran was getting ready for his shift on Sunday night when he got a text from Nicola asking him to come over. Johnny wasn't feeling well and had asked for him. So, by seven thirty he was striding up her path, and she opened the door before he reached the porch step.

"Thank you for coming," she said and ushered him inside. "I said I'd take him to the ER, but he specifically asked if you would come here. I think he has a fever, but he's been running hot and cold all evening. I'm not sure what's wrong."

"No problem," he said and held up his doctor's bag. "I don't start work for another hour. Is he in his room?"

She seemed frazzled. In baggy gray sweats, her hair in an untidy top knot and her cheeks flushed, Kieran thought he'd never seen her look more beautiful, and he fought the urge to haul her into his arms and kiss her like crazy.

"I'll take you up," she said, and he followed her up the stairs.

Marco was on the landing, cheerfully saying how he wasn't sick at all. When they reached Johnny's room, the boy was in bed under the covers, one arm flung over his forehead. He groaned, then made some comment about how his head hurt. Marco was hovering, and Nicola quickly shooed him back to his own room. Kieran examined Johnny, conscious that Nicola was standing by nervously, looking determined to think the worst. She was biting her lip, arms crossed, clearly at breaking point. When the exam was done and Johnny was back under the covers, he looked around the room, making a few observations.

"Okay, I need to speak with your aunt," he told Johnny. "You stay put and we'll be back up in a little while."

Kieran packed up his stethoscope and ushered Nicola from the room. She jabbered on as they headed downstairs and, when they reached the hallway, she grabbed his arms, her fingers digging into his skin.

"Please tell me what's wrong," she implored. "Is it serious? Chicken pox? Measles? Or something worse? Don't tell me—it's something worse," she said and gripped him harder. "He's really sick, isn't he? Kids don't get fevers without a reason. Maybe I didn't make him dress warm enough." Her eyes glistened. "This is my fault. He's really sick, and it's my—"

"He's not sick," Kieran said and grasped her chin, tilting her face up. "He's faking."

Her eyes widened. "Faking?"

"Faking," Kieran said again, rubbing her chin with his thumb. "He has a heating pad tucked under his bed. A minute or two held against the temple and presto… instant fever."

"But why…"

Kieran looked up and spotted both Marco and Johnny at the top of the stairs. They were grinning and whispering and had clearly hatched the plan together.

"That's why," he said and kissed her soundly on the lips. The boys giggled and then raced back to their rooms.

Nicola kissed him back for a moment and pulled away. "Little monsters."

"They just want to see you happy," he said and released her.

"They don't know that you make me miserable."

She was smiling as she spoke, but the words still stung. He remembered what she'd said the day before—about forgetting all about them once they were done. That had stung, too. Enough for him to bail on the party earlier than he'd needed to. "Do I?"

"No," she admitted. "Not really."

"I'm glad," he said. "Now, I need to get out of here before I kiss you again. I'll see you Tuesday."

She wrapped her arms around her waist. "How about tomorrow?" she suggested. "I'm working, so why don't you stop by the restaurant and have dinner?"

Kieran's brows shot up. "That sounds like a date."

"A pizza and bread sticks with me and the boys? If you think that's a date, then you need to get out more," she said and grinned.

Laughter rumbled in his chest. "Ain't that the truth. Okay, tomorrow. See you then." He walked to the door and turned. "And you might want to remove the heating pad from his bed—don't want him burning anything."

She gasped. "God… I don't think I'll ever get this parenting thing right."

"Sure you will," he replied. "You're a natural. All they need is love. And you're good at that."

Something passed between them, a look that spoke volumes, a look that had everything to do with their past and their present. A look that made him want her more than he'd believed possible. She called it unfinished business. He knew that it was simple destiny. An inevitability since they were fifteen years old.

He spent the next twenty-four hours wrapped up in thoughts of her. Jonah called and talked through the proposal for the pond, sending him the plans via email. After an uneventful shift in the ER, Kieran headed to JoJo's around six thirty on Monday evening.

He spotted Nicola the moment he entered. Dressed in a black skirt and white blouse, black pumps and with her hair pulled back, she looked too beautiful for words. He stayed by the bar for a few minutes, watching as she effortlessly did her job, chatting to customers, taking orders, coordinating the staff. She'd left a successful career back in San Francisco, but the work she did now had so much value. Her very presence in the restaurant made people happy. She was in her element, and thinking of how she'd moved her life and embraced looking after her nephews made his admiration for her grow. She had a kind heart and a strength he suspected she didn't know she possessed.

She looked up and met his gaze, her mouth creasing into a smile, and his insides did a crazy leap. Seconds later she was by the bar and lightly pressed a hand onto his forearm. Even through his jacket and shirt, Kieran's skin burned from her touch. But he didn't pull away.

"You're here," she said and removed her hand. "The boys will be happy. They've become very fond of you."

"It's mutual," he admitted and felt the truth of his words hit deep down. "So, are you happy, too?" She shrugged and turned. "I'm happy, too. Come over to the booth, and I'll get you a drink."

"Just club soda," he said and followed her, slipping into the seat.

She smiled. "You're so hard core."

"Yeah, I think we've already discussed how I'm the sweetest guy on the planet."

Her smile widened, and she went to speak but was interrupted by the excited chatter from Marco as he sidled up into the booth, followed closely by his brother. Johnny wasn't quite so animated but managed a grin when Kieran asked how he was feeling now he'd recovered from his fever. Nicola disappeared, and Kieran spent some time chatting to the boys, talking about school and the fishpond and how they wanted a basketball hoop installed in the backyard.

"Do you like kids?" Marco asked, biting into a breadstick.

"Of course he likes kids," Johnny said quickly. "He's here with us. And he's a doctor."

The boy's logic made Kieran grin. "Johnny's right. I like kids."

"Do you like older kids or just babies?" Marco asked, biting his lower lip just like his aunt did.

Johnny groaned impatiently. "Everyone likes babies, stupid. Older kids are the ones who get left."

"Left where?" Marco asked seriously.

"At the place where they leave kids who don't have a mom and a dad," Johnny explained matter-of-factly. "Everyone knows that. There's a girl in my class, and she was festered."

"Festered?" Marco's eyes were as big as saucers.

Kieran bit back a grin. "He means *fostered*," he explained to the younger boy. "Sometimes children who don't have a mom and dad go and live with foster parents."

"But we don't have a mom and dad," Marco stated. "So do we have to go and live with other people?"

"No," Kieran explained quickly. "Because you have

your aunt. You have family who want you to live with them."

Marco relaxed a little. "So, even if Aunt Nicola had her own kids, we could still live with her?"

"Of course," he replied.

"And it doesn't matter that there's no dad?" Marco asked.

Johnny rolled his eyes. "If Aunt Nicola had a baby then there would be a dad—don't you know anything? You gotta have a mom and a dad to make a baby."

"Who says?" Marco asked.

"Everyone. Except for Sissy Culhane—she's another girl in my class. She doesn't have a mom," Johnny said somberly. "But I think her mom died or something."

Kieran had gone to school with Joss Culhane, Sissy's father. "You're right, Sissy's mom died a long time ago."

"I wish my mom hadn't died," Marco said, his lip wobbling. "And my dad. But we're lucky that we've got Aunt Nicola to love us. And when she gets married, we'll have a dad again. Won't we?" he asked, looking at Kieran.

Kieran saw the longing in the boy's eyes, and something uncurled deep down, a feeling he'd pushed away for two years because it hurt too much to think about. Losing Christian had nearly broken him, and he was reluctant to feel that again. But it was hard not to feel the emotional tug that came from spending time with two children who were clearly longing for a father to replace the one they'd tragically lost.

"Yes, one day, perhaps you will," he said quietly.

"You could marry her." Johnny suggested and shrugged.

Kieran's skin burned. Yes, he could. But he wasn't about to say that. "Well, I'm not sure I—"

"Don't you want to marry her?" Marco asked, eyes wide. "Why not? I mean, she's pretty, right?"

Kieran tugged at his collar. "Yes, she's very pretty."

"And smart," Johnny added. "And she makes the best spaghetti and meatballs ever."

"You're right," Kieran said in agreement. "She does."

"Do you know anyone else who could marry Aunt Nicola?" Marco asked and chewed his lip some more. "And it would have to be someone we liked. And who liked us."

"What about the guy who came to check out the yard for the fishpond?" Johnny asked and chugged on some soda the waitress had delivered.

Jonah? Yeah…maybe not. "I don't think so."

"Maybe the policeman," Johnny said and then cast his eyes down guiltily. "The one who phoned Aunt Nicola about me."

Hank Culhane? "No," Kieran said and sipped his drink.

"But policemen like kids," Marco mused. "So do firemen. Do you know any firemen?"

"Why do you need a fireman?" Nicola's voice instantly cut through the chatter. "Is there a fire?"

Only the one in Kieran's belly when he thought about Nicola being with another man. He plastered on a smile. "Just boy talk," he quipped and shrugged. "So, I thought we were having pizza tonight?"

The moment he spoke, a waitress appeared and a family-sized tray was placed on the table. Nicola slid into the booth beside him, and he caught the scent of her perfume as she edged closer.

"Okay, dig in," she said and grabbed a slice of pizza.

The boys followed suit, and then Kieran helped himself.

"So why were you three talking about firemen?" she asked.

"We're trying to find you a husband," Marco announced, and Kieran saw her jaw drop. "So that Johnny and I won't end up in that place where the kids without a mom and dad go."

"What place?" she echoed, and then her voice got louder. "And what husband?"

"A husband for you," Johnny said and shrugged. "One that can give you a baby."

"How would the baby get inside your belly, Aunt Nicola?" Marco asked, wide-eyed.

Kieran fidgeted in his seat. The conversation was going from bad to worse. He looked sideways, saw the mortified expression on her face and managed a wry grin. "Haven't had The Talk yet, huh?"

"Of course not," she replied. "They're eight and ten."

"And curious," he said quietly. "Better start talking."

"You're the doctor," she reminded him, a deep scarlet hue crawling up her neck. "And much more qualified for it than me."

"Oh, no…you're the parent. This one's all yours."

"Please," she begged. He looked at her, saw her lip tremble and took pity on her. "Okay. But you owe me for this."

Kieran spent the next fifteen minutes explaining conception and childbirth to the boys, answering their questions as they shoved pizza into their mouths and drank soda. When he was done, Marco looked at him thoughtfully and asked another question.

"So, could *you* give Aunt Nicola a baby?"

"Well, I… I…"

His voice trailed off, and she sucked in a breath and jumped in to save him. "Who wants more pizza?"

The question quickly forgotten, the boys shook their heads and pleaded to leave the table and head upstairs to watch television. Once they were gone, she leaned closer and spoke. "I bet right now you're wanting to call the fire department."

He smiled wryly. "Thanks for the help. Next time you're on your own."

She laughed and moved back. "Sorry about that... looks like the boys have you set in their sights."

"I could think of worse fates," he said and finished his drink.

"I guess that only means one thing," she said quietly.

He stilled. "And what's that?"

She slid from the booth and got to her feet. "That we're in big trouble."

Chapter Nine

Nicola was driving back from one of the local produce farms early the following afternoon, when she was delayed just before the bridge for over an hour while the police and paramedics cleared an accident scene. From the mangled vehicle being hauled by a tow truck, the amount of debris on the road and the wailing sirens, it looked bad and, when she finally picked the boys up from school, she gave them an extralong hug.

She headed to the restaurant, had a debrief with the assistant manager and did inventory on the bar. Once she was done, she left the boys with her father for the evening and then headed home to shower and change. She had a date with Kieran. Okay…not a date. A few hours of unfinished business. But she intended following through with it.

By the time she tapped on his door, it was nearly eight o'clock. The door swung back, and he looked surprised to see her.

"Oh…Nic. Hey."

He seemed distracted, out of sorts, and she frowned. "Everything all right?"

"Sure," he said and opened the door wider, ushering her inside. "Would you like a drink?"

He had already closed the door and was striding down the narrow hallway before she responded. "Okay. Wine if you have it."

"Of course," he said and rummaged through a couple of cupboards for a glass.

She stripped off her coat and dropped her tote, feeling the warmth of the central heating seep through to her bones. She got a good look at him and realized he was still wearing his work clothes. And he looked terrible. "Long day?"

He poured the wine and glanced up. "You could say that."

His weary expression was unmissable. "What happened?"

She took the glass he offered and waited. He let out a long breath, met her gaze and spoke quietly. "I lost someone today."

"Someone?"

"A patient," he explained. "A seventeen-year-old girl involved in an MVA."

Nicola's insides crunched up. "I'm so sorry. I think I was caught up in the traffic jam from that accident today. It happened just before the bridge, right?"

He nodded. "Single vehicle. Texting while driving. She sustained significant chest and head injuries." He ran a weary hand over his face. "God, it was just awful. There were two other girls in the car who survived... but damn, I couldn't save her. I tried. I tried so freakin' hard. But it wasn't enough."

Nicola's eyes burned, and she blinked the tears away. "I'm sure you did everything you could."

He shrugged. "Doesn't mean squat, though, particularly when I had to tell her parents. Her father was inconsolable. Her mother hauntingly silent. And, as the words were coming out of my mouth, I kept thinking, what do I know about real loss? Raising a child for seventeen years, then losing them because of a damned text message…that's about as real and extreme as it gets."

She nodded, because she had no idea what to say to him. And then she found her voice. "I imagine that it never gets easier."

His gaze narrowed. "Telling loved ones that they've lost someone? No, never. And while I was doing it, while I was watching these people suffer through the terrible news, I thought, is this what my parents felt when Liz died? Is this what your father felt when Gino was killed? And how did the person telling them really feel? I felt sorry for myself. And angry at this teenager whose heart was literally in my hands as I was trying to revive her. I kept thinking, how could she do this, how could she choose to send a text message and hurt these people so much?"

Nicola placed her glass on the counter, moved around to get closer to Kieran and rested her hands on his shoulders, looking up into his eyes. "Because that's what real life is. It's hurt and loss, and sometimes it just sucks. But I'll bet that someday, when they can look back on the moment clearly, her parents will be grateful that it was you who told them she had passed away and that it was done with compassion and kindness and with real feeling."

He sighed and dropped his chin to the top of her head, wrapping his arms around her. "Thank you," he whispered. "I'm glad you're here. You look amazing, by the way."

She smiled gently and pulled back, touching his face.

"You don't. You look wrecked. Why don't you have a shower and get changed, and I'll cook something, since you probably haven't eaten."

He nodded and expelled a heavy breath. "You're right. I need to get out of these clothes. Be back in ten."

Once he left the room, Nicola took a sip of wine and then rummaged through the refrigerator, finding eggs and peppers and cheddar, and set about making an omelet. As she cracked and whisked the eggs, it occurred to her how neat and tidy the place was. The apartment looked even tidier than when Kayla had occupied it. She found sourdough on the countertop and cut a few thick slices for toast and waited for him to return before she put the ingredients in the pan.

When he walked back down the hall about fifteen minutes later, he was showered, shaved and dressed. Well, half-dressed. He wore low-riding jeans with the top button undone and a white T-shirt that amplified the broadness of his shoulders and clung to a good portion of his muscular chest. His feet were bare, his hair damp, and the scent of whatever cologne he used assailed her immediately, shooting her libido up like a firecracker, and she tossed back the rest of the wine.

The temperature in the room seemed to hike a few degrees, and she waved a hand. "Um…food. It won't take long."

"Don't go to any trouble."

"No trouble," she insisted. "You know I like to cook. And my dad rarely lets me into the kitchen at the restaurant. He likes to supervise the chef," she said and grinned.

"You do a good job," he remarked and came around the counter. "Being in charge suits you."

"Because I'm bossy?"

"Exactly," he said and grinned. "Sorry I wasn't in a good place when I answered the door."

She raised a brow. "You forget I was coming over?"

He shrugged lightly. "Not really... I just didn't think, if that makes sense."

"Perfect sense," she replied and began making the omelet. "Incidentally, are you a neat freak or something? There's nothing out of place here."

He grinned. "Not quite. The old lady downstairs comes up and cleans for me every Monday. She has a daughter in Idaho who gives her grief and needs the money, and I..." His words trailed off and he shrugged again. "You know...just trying to help."

He really is the most perfect human being in the universe.

The moment the thought came into her head, Nicola wanted to get it out. But she couldn't.

"I wish you were flawed."

He laughed, and the sound warmed her blood. "I am," he assured her. "You know that better than anyone."

She shrugged one shoulder. "High school was a long time ago. We've both grown up since then. And I know why you did it the way you did."

"Because you wouldn't have accepted it any other way," he replied, confirming her suspicions. "I had to hurt you back then. I had to make you hate me. If we'd tried doing things long-distance, it would have dragged out and become a great big mess. I didn't want that for you, Nic. I cared about you too much."

"I know," she said, her throat closing over, her eyes burning. "We both wanted different things. I knew how important medical school was to you, and I know I would have made it difficult for you to concentrate on studying if we'd stayed together and were living in different states. We were too young for that kind of commitment."

He nodded. "But I am truly sorry for hurting you. And I'm sorry that your fiancé was a jerk and didn't realize what he had. You deserve better."

Tears plumped at the corners of her eyes, and she quickly blinked them away, skillfully flipping the omelet. "I guess I'm just not the marrying kind."

"Sure you are," he said and shrugged loosely.

"If only there was a fireman handy," she said and pushed the bread into the toaster.

Color slashed his cheeks. "I'm sure they're overrated."

"Yeah," she said and grinned. "All those muscles and rescuing kittens from trees. So overrated."

He chuckled, and the sound warmed her through to the soles of her feet. Despite the undercurrent of sexual awareness between them, there was something else, something even more powerful. Friendship. Trust. Companionship. It had built steadily over the past couple of weeks. And it wasn't new. It wasn't some passing fancy. It was built on the foundation of their teenage romance. It was about knowing they were so important to one another back then. And in some ways, that friendship hadn't faded, not through years apart, or angry words or bitterness and hurt. It was in a kind of limbo, waiting to be unwrapped and given new life.

She nibbled on a piece of buttered toast while he ate, not wanting to make him feel self-conscious. And they talked…about the boys, and their work now and the work they'd left behind. They talked about Gino and Miranda and Liz, and he admitted to finding it hard to forgive his father for betraying his mother and for

Jonah's very existence. And they talked about the accident and the patient he'd lost.

And then he talked about his son.

"I can't imagine how hard it was for you."

He sighed heavily. "Honestly…it was as though I had my heart ripped out. He was my child. Or so I believed. And it still hurts so much."

He bared his feelings in a way she suspected he'd never done before, and his blue eyes had never glittered more brightly.

"I'm so sorry."

He nodded. "When you love someone that much and they're taken from you, it's like a wound that never heals. And I'm terrified of…" His words trailed off and he shook his head. "You know."

"Loving anyone again?" she prompted. "Loving a child again?"

"Yes," he admitted.

Nicola's throat closed over and she swallowed hard. Then she grabbed his hand and got to her feet, dragging him with her. She didn't have to speak. They didn't need any more words. He linked their fingers intimately and led her down the hall and into the bedroom.

The huge bed filled the room, and the bedside lamp gave enough light to dapple his skin. He took an unopened box of condoms from the drawer and ripped open the box. Then he pulled off his T-shirt immediately and moved in front of her, undoing the buttons on her dress one at a time, the back of his fingers skimming over her skin. Once the buttons were dealt with, the dress slipped over her shoulders and onto the floor. Her breasts surged, spilling over the top of the white lace bra, her nipples straining through the soft fabric. His gaze swept over her, past her breasts, down her rib cage and stomach, over the white panties and down to her thighs and then back up.

"You're so beautiful, Nic," he rasped. "I feel like it's our first time all over again."

It was quite the admission, and she realized that he was just as vulnerable as she was. His honesty was a powerful aphrodisiac, giving her strength, but also grabbing like fingers around her heart. And she knew, in that moment, that it would never be just sex between them. There were too many feelings. Too much history. Too much love...

I'm still in love with him...

The realization should have sent her running. But she wasn't going to deny her body and heart what it craved. It was one night. A few hours. The two of them. Their past now meeting their present.

She slowly unclipped her bra, freeing her breasts, watching his visual appraisal with a surge of resolve and desire. Shoes and underwear quickly followed and, once she was naked, she tossed her hair back and took a long breath. "Make love to me."

He groaned, curling a hand around her neck and threading his fingers through her hair, anchoring her head. And then he was kissing her—long, hot and deep kisses that went beyond any they'd shared before. Nicola touched his chest, running eager hands all over him, feeling his smooth skin, seeking out sensitive places with her fingertips. She undid his fly and pushed the jeans down over his hips, and he took about two seconds to flick them off. And then they were naked together, breasts to chest, hip to hip, thigh to thigh. He kissed her again, slower, deeper, hotter and hotter with each passing moment. Nicola grabbed his shoulders, hanging on while he effortlessly carried her to the bed and, once they were lying together, his magic fingers went to work, finding her wet and ready for him.

But he took his time kissing her, anointing every part of her skin with his mouth, teasing her breasts with his tongue before taking an aching nipple into his mouth. Nicola pushed her hands into his hair, urging him, wanting him, feverish and desperate to feel him inside her.

"Please," she begged, dragging his lips to hers so she could feel the seductive thrust of his tongue in her mouth. "I want to feel you inside me."

"Soon, very soon," he promised, trailing his mouth down her rib cage and farther still, until finally he was between her thighs, driving her insane with such skillful prowess that she gasped his name over and over. It was insanely erotic, the most intense feeling she had experienced in her life. He continued his exploration, his hands gently stroking her breasts, his mouth on the most intimate part of her, and Nicola grabbed his shoulders and clung to him, shuddering as wave after wave of pleasure coursed through her.

And then, when the shudders stopped and her breathing came back to earth, he grabbed the foil packet he'd placed on the bedside table, ripped it open and rolled the condom in place. When he moved over her, resting his weight on his arms, his erection seeking entrance, she welcomed him, parting her thighs as she grabbed his hips and drew him intimately inside.

It was like it had always been between them. Two people who knew one another perfectly. He kissed her deeply, seeking out her tongue, tasting her as he moved, creating a steady, erotic rhythm she knew would bring them both release. But he took more time because, at that moment, it felt as though they had all the time in the world. No one would dare intrude. Their hips met each other, thrust for thrust, his hands in her hair, mouths hovering close together, sighing, breathing, faster and faster. And when they could take no more, they both rose up and into that place where only pleasure existed. They came together, sharp and intense and on a wave of white-hot release so overpowering it shook them both to the very core.

When it was over, he rolled off her, his breathing ragged, his chest rising and falling. He got up and disappeared into the bathroom, returning seconds later. Nicola didn't bother to hide her nakedness, since he'd seen all of her there was to see.

"Well," she said as he flopped back onto the bed and pulled the duvet up. "That was good."

"Good?" he queried, his eyes shut.

She chuckled. "Okay…great. The best ever. You've learned a thing or two since high school."

Laughter rumbled in his chest. "I needed to."

Nicola rolled and traced her fingertips through the light dusting of hair on his chest. "Oh, I don't know, we made out okay back then. Unless you have some other tricks in your repertoire?"

He gently grabbed a handful of her hair and found her mouth, kissing her. "I just might."

"Care to elaborate?"

He rolled, taking her with him, pinning her to the bed, his eyes never bluer. "You bet."

He spent the next two hours elaborating. They touched, they kissed, they talked and laughed, and Nicola experienced a connection she'd never felt before. It was rediscovery all over again—only this time, they were older, bolder and wiser. And finally, when they were both sated and exhausted, they fell asleep, spoon fashion. When she awoke, it was after six, and she caught a sliver of morning sun slicing through the curtains. She slipped out of bed and found her clothes, dressed quickly and then headed to the kitchen to make coffee.

And she thought long and hard about what she'd done.

She'd fallen back in love with Kieran. Big mistake.

She'd fallen back into his bed. Bigger mistake.

And now she had to work out a way to get out of it.

He'd made it abundantly clear that he was in no position to have a serious relationship. And she wouldn't accept anything less. She'd be a rebound relationship at best. And Nicola wasn't ever going to put herself in that place again. Because there was nothing nice about being someone's *convenience*. The next time she gave her heart, she wanted a heart in return.

He was still in bed when she returned to the bedroom, lying on his stomach, his face buried in the pillow. The duvet had slipped and exposed his back, and her fingers itched with the urge to touch him.

"I've brought coffee," she said and placed the mug on the bedside next to a significantly less full box of condoms. "It's time to wake up."

He groaned into the pillow. "Come back to bed."

"I can't," Nicola said. "I have to pick the kids up and get them ready for school."

He rolled and grabbed her hand, urging her to sit on the edge of the bed. "Can I see you tonight?"

"I'm working," she replied.

"Tomorrow?"

"Same."

His gaze narrowed. "So, you've had your wicked way with me, and now we're done?"

Nicola shrugged. "Well, that was the deal."

He pulled himself into a sitting position. "Seriously?"

She stepped back from the bed and propped her hands on her hips. "I don't want to have illusions about this, Kieran. I have to think about what's best for the boys and—let's face it—anyone you get involved with is going to be a rebound relationship."

"Rebound? That's ridiculous."

She shook her head. "It's not. Admit it. You only stopped wearing your wedding band a few months ago."

"Because of my—"

"I know why," she said, pushing air into her lungs, trying to stay strong. "Because it helped you stay connected to someone you loved. Someone you still love. I get it. But I've been that transitional girl before, and I don't want to be it again. I can't afford to, not when I have the boys to think about. They need stability, and they need me to be whole and functional and not in the middle of some messy, half-baked relationship with a man who still has feelings for someone else."

He swung his legs off the bed. "I'm not still in love with my ex-wife."

"Are you sure?" she shot back, aching inside. "Your body may be here, Kieran...but I think a big part of your heart is back in Sioux Falls."

"You're being—"

"Realistic," she said, cutting him off. "And this is what I want. We agreed to have sex and get each other out of our systems, and we did. It was great. It was fun. It was exactly what we needed to do."

He got up, grabbed a pair of sweats from the chair in the corner and slipped them on. "You didn't respond like you were trying to get me out of your system, Nic. You responded like you couldn't get enough. And I'll bet that if I took you in my arms and kissed you right now, we'd be in that bed within two seconds, and you'd be screaming my name."

"I can't believe you just said that."

"It's the truth."

"Your truth," she shot back.

He rolled his eyes. "Are we really going to have a fight about this?"

"Sei incredibile," she hissed. "I also can't believe I let you touch me."

"Believe it," he shot back. "I've got a half-empty box of condoms to prove it."

Nicola cursed at him again, grabbed her jacket, spun on her heels and strode from the room. By the time she reached the living room, she was so mad she was shaking. She grabbed her tote and headed for the front door. She slammed it on her way out—hard and with purpose—and barely took a breath until she reached her car. But she didn't expect to find Kieran chasing after her, wearing only his sweats, clearly stumbling over the gravel driveway for the last half a dozen steps.

"Would you stop being so ridiculous and come back inside?" he demanded. "It's freezing out here."

Nicola glared at him, ignoring the fact he was half-naked and standing on the sidewalk and that he had a mark on his neck that looked suspiciously like a hickey. Well, served him right!

"I'd have to be a fool to dive back into bed with you," she said and opened her car door.

"Nic...please?"

"Don't call me that," she said and glared at him. "Don't call me anything. Just don't call me!"

"You came here, remember?" he reminded her. "To my apartment. Twice in one week. And you asked me to make love to you. If anyone's done the chasing here, it's you."

She burned hot from head to toe. "You're such a conceited ass!"

He laughed humorlessly. "So, this is it? We're done?"

"Yes," she said, dumping her tote onto the passenger seat. "You couldn't be any more out of my system than you are right now."

Getting back into the car, she drove off, refusing to look back in case she spotted him in the rearview mirror. If she had her way, she'd never see him again.

She drove home, cursing that it was only two streets and didn't take long enough for her to have let off all the steam churning through her blood. She quickly showered and changed and then headed to JoJo's. The boys were eating breakfast with her father, and Salvatore immediately sensed something was wrong because he told his grandsons to stay in the kitchen and finish their breakfast.

"Everything okay, *bella*?"

"Fine, Papa," she lied. "Just a lot on my mind. Thank you for watching the boys again."

"Bad date?" he asked and grinned.

"The worst," she replied. "What makes you say that, though?

He chuckled. "You have that look. Did you know your mama wouldn't go out with me the first time I asked her? She said I was too arrogant. Too sure of myself."

Nicola knew the story well. "But she chose you in the end."

"Exactly," he said, still grinning. "It's not where you start that counts…it's where you end up."

"That doesn't make any sense," she said.

"Of course it does, *bella*," he said more seriously. "You think all matters of the heart are logical. They are not. I saw you the other night with Kieran," he said, reminding her what she'd once felt—what she *still* felt— for the man she knew she had to get out of her system. "I saw you laughing and joking and looking like you used to…not like you have the world pressing down on your shoulders."

"I don't feel like that," she denied, heat burning her eyes. "I'm happy, Papa… I promise."

Her father, usually a man of few words, gently patted her arm. "You have done a good thing here. You have stepped up to care for your nephews, you have taken over running this place and you do a wonderful job. But remember that it is important to have a life of your own, too, hmm?"

"I will, I promise," she said, taking a deep breath.

Twenty minutes later, she was back home, and the boys were getting ready for school. By eight thirty, she drove them to class and had a quick meeting with Johnny's teacher. Even though the charges from the bakery incident had been dropped, she'd informed the school about his behavior, wanting to ensure he wasn't also misbehaving in class. And his teacher was understanding and supportive of her decision not to ground him. Johnny had been through enough. She made another appointment to catch up again with the teacher at the end of the week and once she had finished with the meeting, Nicola returned to town. There was a tour bus arriving at midday, and she talked through the menu with the chef before heading out to do the banking and settle a few accounts.

Her day dragged. Kieran was due to spend some time with Marco the following day, but she doubted he'd show. She suspected he'd pull out of the Big Brothers, too.

Good.

She didn't want to see him again. She didn't want any more reminders about how stupidly she'd behaved, or how *over* they really were. It was time she pulled herself together and forgot all about him. If she was ever going to move on, Nicola knew she had to let go of their past once and for all.

On Thursday morning, she had a coffee date planned with Connie and headed to the O'Sullivan hotel around eleven. Before she even made it to the elevator, she'd bumped into Gwen. She wondered if the older woman had some kind of sixth sense and she dragged an unresisting Nicola into the restaurant. Once they were seated and sipping cappuccinos, Gwen spoke, her expression kind and generous.

"You look like you need a friend," the older woman remarked. "Or a mom."

Tears sprang to her eyes, and Nicola swallowed hard. She didn't want to do this. She didn't want to fall apart in front of Kieran's mother. But good intentions flew out the window the moment Gwen patted her hand.

"I don't know what to do," she said and sighed. "I'm trying to keep it all together...to be a good parent to the boys, to run the restaurant, to have a life. But I feel as though I'm failing at most of those things."

"You're not," Gwen assured her. "Being a parent is hard work, but you'll get better at it as time moves along. Is there anything else?" the older woman asked. "Something else bothering you?"

"You mean a six-foot-two something," she admitted and expelled a heavy breath. "I don't know how to stop."

"Stop?"

"Being in love with your son," she said, her heart aching.

Gwen's mouth curled into a gentle smile. "Perhaps you're not meant to."

She shrugged. "Maybe. But it hurts when the person you love doesn't love you in return."

"Are you so sure that he doesn't?" Gwen asked.

Nicola nodded. "He's not ready for this...for us... for the boys. And I can't accept anything less than everything, not when I have two children to consider. If it was only me," she said and shrugged, "who knows, maybe I'd take the risk. But the kids already have him earmarked to make a great husband and father, and—"

"They're right," Gwen said and regarded her seriously. "My son is an incredible man. He's kind and compassionate and strong, and he *was* a good husband and a wonderful father. Losing all that broke something inside of him. But seeing you together...seeing him with your nephews and with you, it's obvious that the four of you belong together."

It was a nice, romantic idea, but Nicola wasn't convinced. She knew the boys would relish the idea, but it was a fantasy. They'd agreed to keep it casual, to purge any lingering feelings they had for one another. But it had spectacularly backfired. He wanted no-strings sex. She wanted a lifetime commitment.

"Liam said I was Kieran's Kryptonite," Nicola said quietly. "But I think that perhaps that's what we are to each other...it seems like a good idea but, for some reason, it just doesn't work."

"He's been hurt in the past," Gwen reminded her. "Badly. And he's terrified of that happening again. Can you blame him?"

"No," she replied. "But I don't want to be his rebound affair, either. I've been there before, and it's not a lot of fun."

"No, it's not," Gwen agreed. "I was married to a man for thirty-five years who was in love with someone else for most of that time…but I don't think that's your fate. I think you'll get the life you want."

Nicola wasn't so sure. "I want so many things. But right now, I'd settle for not feeling so unhappy."

Gwen smiled. "Don't give up on him, Nicola. He's worth fighting for."

"You're biased," she said and half shrugged.

"Of course. But you know I'm right."

She did. Because Kieran was worth fighting for. But she was, too…and that was want she wanted. His fight. His belief that they were more than simply a chemical reaction to one another. More than an itch needing to be scratched for a few hours. More than a memory.

She wanted his love.

But he had a mountain of insecurities to scale before she would let him into her heart ever again.

Chapter Ten

"So, are you and your girlfriend in the middle of some sort of crisis?"

Kieran stared his brother, ignored the question and kept walking around the garden. Nicola's garden. She was inside, working on the accounts for JoJo's. But knowing her as he did, there had to be steam coming out of her ears—he was sure of it.

Jonah grinned. "She's got spirit, that's for sure."

"She's not my girlfriend. She's not my anything," he said pointedly and waved the plans in front of his brother's face. "Can we get back to this?"

It was Friday afternoon and the second time he'd been at her house since Tuesday. The day before, he'd arrived to spend time with Marco, and she'd barely spared him a glance, muttering something about expecting him to bail. And he almost had. He'd almost pulled the plug on having anything to do with her, her nephews or the damned fishpond. But his conscience had given him grief and, in the end, he knew he didn't have the heart to disappoint the boys. It wasn't their fault that he and their aunt were having a…thing. And now they were happily shooting baskets through the new basketball hoop he'd fixed to the side of the shed the day before.

"Yeah…she's not anything. That's why you look as though you want to punch someone."

"Are you volunteering?"

Jonah laughed, which was unexpected, since he rarely looked anything other than moody and resentful. "Keep me out of your romance problems." He walked on ahead and then turned. "So, what did you do?"

"Do?"

There was another clang in the kitchen. "Yeah, *do*. You obviously screwed up."

Kieran's mouth twisted. "She's impossible."

"And you expected something different?" Jonah queried.

"I expect rational behavior. I expect to know what I've done wrong."

"From the woman you're in love with?" his brother said bluntly.

"I'm not in love with her," he denied and strode around the yard, standing in front of the spot where the pond would go.

"Sure you are," Jonah said and grinned for a second. "Not that it's any of my business. But Liam thinks you never stopped loving her. And since she's inside hating you, you should probably go in there and talk it out."

Kieran scowled. "Stay out of it. You *and* Liam."

"I'm out," Jonah said. "Just a little brotherly concern."

Kieran made an exasperated sound, shoved the plans into Jonah's hands and trudged up to the house, making his way into the kitchen. She was at the dining table, tapping keys on the laptop. Her hair was up, and he caught a glimpse of one shoulder as her loose sweater dipped to the left. He swallowed hard, trying to think about anything other than her skin, her scent, or the way she moved. But it was impossible. Everything about her affected him on some primary, soul-reaching level. If he had any sense, he'd ignore her bad mood, stride directly toward her and haul her into his arms and kiss her beautiful neck.

"What do you want?" she asked, not looking at him, but clearly sensing his presence.

Kieran moved into the kitchen and placed a hand on the countertop. "Just letting you know there'll be contractors here on Tuesday to dig out the hole for the pond."

"I'll write a check to cover it," she said, still not looking at him.

"It was my idea," he reminded her. "I'll pay for it."

"I'm not a charity case."

"No," he said, suddenly all out of patience. "At the moment you're a head case."

She jumped to her feet and jammed her hands onto her hips.

"Jerk."

Kieran sucked in a breath. "Why are you so angry?"

"You know why."

He shrugged. "If I did, I doubt we'd be having this conversation. You're the one who bailed the other day."

She glared at him. "*I'm* the one who bailed. *I'm* the one who chased you. I guess it's all on me."

"Let's get this straight," he said and moved closer toward her, crossing him arms. "You're angry because I pointed out the obvious?"

"I'm angry at myself," she shot back. "Not you."

"Sure doesn't seem like it."

"Not everything is about you," she said hotly. "I

realized I made a mistake and shouldn't have gotten involved, okay?"

"Is this because you think I'm still in love with my ex-wife?" he asked quickly. "Because I assure you, that's not the case."

"Then who are you in love with?"

Kieran rocked back on his heels, a rush of words surging through his blood, but none would come out. Suddenly he knew what she wanted…knew what she expected…but he couldn't admit what he was feeling. It was too early. Too raw. Too risky. And he wasn't ready for any declarations.

"Nic, I…"

"Exactly," she said and shrugged. "You can't. You're not ready. You're nowhere near ready. And as much as you want to deny it, you are still wrapped up in your ex-wife," she said and then raised a hand when he went to protest. "And, yeah, maybe it's not love. Maybe it's other feelings, other emotions…but they are still there. Still haunting you. Still making it impossible for you to move on."

Resentment sparked in his chest, heating his blood. "Okay," he said and waved an exasperated hand. "So, maybe I'm not ready for some huge commitment. But I'm ready to spend time with you and be with you and—"

"Sleep with me?" she added. "Yeah, I know. Just sex. No strings, remember."

"They were *your* words," he reminded her. "Not mine. You wanted to get me out of your system so *you* could move on. That's what you said. You wanted to get past us. That's why you came to my apartment. That's why you asked me to make love to you. And now you want—what? Something else? Something more? Or what?" He laughed humorlessly. "Consider yourself moved on, I guess."

She had tears in her eyes, but he wasn't swayed. He was pissed. He felt manipulated and betrayed. He'd trusted her to be honest and upfront, and now she was asking for something he wasn't ready to give. He'd had enough of this game.

"I'd like you to leave," she said and turned away. "I'll tell the boys you had to go. And take your brother with you."

"That's your answer? Kicking me out?"

She made a miffed sound. "I'm not going to waste any more time on you *or* us."

Kieran didn't hang around. What he wanted to do was go to O'Sullivan's and throw down a few shots of bourbon to help ease the rage and confusion coursing through his blood. But, since he was on call for the next three days, he headed home, slumped in front of the television and drank a cola.

His cell pinged, and he stared at the number. Nicola. He looked at the message.

Flowers would be nice. N

Flowers? Was she serious? Didn't they just break up? Not that they were together...but it sure felt like a breakup. He dumped the phone onto the sofa and stared at the television.

Damned if he'd be a part of anymore female manipulation. He'd spent too many years married to someone who had lied to his face over and over, pretending to want him, making him love a child who wasn't his. He wasn't going to be that stupid again. Or that gullible. His next relationship—if there was a next one—would be on his terms. And that meant he wasn't about to get sucked in by Nicola's hot-and-cold routine. She either wanted him or she didn't.

It would be his way or the highway.

He wouldn't be swayed. He couldn't be. Because he wasn't in love with her. Sure, he wanted her. And making love with her had been incredible. They had great chemistry.

And, of course, he *liked* her. They had a lot of history. A lot in common. He enjoyed being around her. He couldn't get enough of her scent, her smile, the damned sexy way she swayed when she walked. Kissing her was like nothing he'd ever experienced.

And he liked being around the kids, too, even though it was the last thing he'd imagined he'd want to do. And maybe the hurt he'd felt over losing Christian had lessened some since he'd been spending time with Marco and Johnny.

And maybe, the more time he spent with Nicola, his heart didn't feel like it was closed for business. Perhaps there were times over the past few weeks when he had stopped being afraid to actually feel something for someone, in case it was cruelly taken away.

He was conflicted. Because he wanted to be with her, but didn't know how to on her terms. She wanted so much more than he was ready to give.

Kieran glanced at the text message again. Was she trying to meet him halfway? To let him know they weren't as over as she had made out. It ignited something in his chest. Relief. Curiosity. Hope.

But I do not love her...

Still, that didn't stop him from heading to a florist in town first thing Saturday morning.

* * *

"Um…there's a big bunch on flowers on the bar with your name on them," Connie said early Saturday afternoon. "So, spill?"

Nicola shrugged and continued filling the salt grinders. Her friend had stopped by the restaurant to drop off more flyers for the rodeo, which was the following weekend. It was one of the major events on the calendar, with competitors coming from around the state to compete for their share of the purse and trophies. There would be a band and dancing and a variety of food and drink vendors, a Ferris wheel and fireworks later in the evening. Of course, the boys wanted to go. And she'd agreed to attend with one of the other parents at school—a single dad who seemed nice and had two young boys of his own. His name was Alex, and she'd bumped into him on Thursday evening at a parent-teacher conference at the school. They'd started talking and, before she knew it, she was agreeing to a date.

Not that it was really a date. But it would be nice to have some *new* adult male company for a change.

And it would help erase a *certain person* from her thoughts.

Because she was tired of thinking about Kieran. Exhausted from too little sleep and too many dreams.

"Nicola?" Connie prompted. "The flowers?"

She shrugged. "O'Sullivan. He's lost his mind."

"What does the card say?"

She mulled over the words for a few seconds. "*As requested.* And then just his initial. And before you ask, I have no idea what it means."

"Did you ask him?" Connie inquired, her eyes wide.

"Of course not," she replied.

"Why not?"

"Because I've misplaced my cell phone and don't know his number." She wasn't about to admit that she suspected she'd left her cell phone at his apartment.

Connie's mouth curved. "I have his number. I can give it to you. And you could always call the hospital?" Connie suggested.

"I know I could," she said. "But I don't want to. I don't want to see him. Talk to him. Touch him. Kiss him. Or anything. Ever again."

Connie's mouth twitched. "Those are some pretty specific things."

"Precisely. And I don't want his stupid flowers."

Her friend grinned. "It's kind of romantic."

Nicola rolled her eyes. "I thought you were on my side. Even though I know you adore the O'Sullivans."

"Not all of them," Connie said pointedly. "But I do like Kieran, and he clearly likes you."

Yeah, sure he does.

But that wasn't enough. Nicola wasn't going to be anyone's second fiddle ever again. Or anyone's consolation prize. He'd made it clear he wasn't up for anything serious and, with the boys to consider, she wasn't about to play roulette with their fragile emotions. Or her own.

"I hate him. End of story."

"Sure you do," Connie said, eyebrows angled. "You're completely in hate with him."

She scowled at her friend. "How about we talk about you and Jonah?"

Connie took about ten seconds to bail.

Nicola spent most of the weekend at the restaurant, other than Sunday afternoon watching a movie with Johnny. Her oldest nephew had opened up a lot in the past week and wasn't as moody and sullen as he'd been in the past. She'd made him apologize to the owner of the bakery, and the older man had agreed to Johnny doing some chores around the place a couple of afternoons after school when the repairs were complete. His accomplice had been forced to do the same thing. His friend didn't seem like a bad kid either, and she'd tentatively agreed to let the boys continue their friendship sometime in the future.

She took some time off on Monday and spent the morning doing a few errands. When she got home, there was a large basket on her doorstep filled with an assortment of candy and wrapped in clear cellophane. There was a card, and she recognized Kieran's scrawl immediately.

For you... K.

Flowers and chocolate? What was he thinking?

She fought the overwhelming urge to confront him but decided the best defense was to ignore him completely. The boys were delighted by the candy, giggling their way through a bar of peppermint chocolate when they got home from school. The babysitter arrived. Mrs. Holden lived down the street, was a widow and had no problem staying with the boys until Nicola returned from the restaurant the few nights a week she worked. It meant her nephews weren't constantly traveling back and forth between the restaurant and the house during school nights.

On Tuesday, the contractors arrived, and she knew Kieran had dropped by because he'd left a note taped to her door informing her of the contractor's schedule. He'd also left a copy of the plans for her and said he'd stop by on Thursday to spend time with Marco and Johnny.

That meant she should make herself scarce. When she arrived home from the restaurant on Thursday night, Mrs. Holden's green Ford sedan was nowhere to be seen. But Kieran's Jeep was parked out by the curb. She stalked up the path, opened the door and found him in the living room, television on, feet up on the coffee table.

And asleep.

She pushed his shoulder to wake him, and he opened his eyes instantly and pulled his feet off the coffee table. "Hey, you're back."

"Where's Mrs. Holden?"

"She had a bad headache, so I sent her home."

Of course he did. "Where are the boys?"

"In bed and asleep. School night, remember?"

Nicola's belly rolled over. He looked so gorgeous with his nut-brown tousled hair and whiskery shadow along his jaw. In jeans and a gray Henley shirt, he looked so hot he could have melted butter.

"You should have—"

"I tried to call your cell, but it went to voice mail," he offered and clicked the TV volume down as he got to his feet.

"I misplaced my cell last week," she explained. "I'm using my spare. I thought I might have left it at your apartment."

He frowned. "You texted me Friday *and* Monday on that cell."

"No," she insisted and searched for her spare phone in her tote. "I didn't."

"The flowers…" His voice trailed off. "You told me you liked flowers. And then I received another one saying you liked candy."

"I did no such thing," she said hotly. "I don't understand how that could—"

"Of course," he said quickly and ran a weary hand through his hair. "The boys."

She stared at him. "Huh?"

"You said you lost your cell phone. They must have taken it and sent the messages."

"They stole my phone?" She was horrified. "And sent you messages to buy me flowers and chocolate?"

"Looks like it."

He was smiling, but Nicola saw nothing funny about the situation. "It didn't occur to you that I would never do that?"

He shrugged. "I thought you were...you know...flirting."

"Why would I do that?" she demanded, turning hot all over.

"Because you want me," he replied casually. "Why else?"

Heat scorched her cheeks. "I don't want you. I don't want anything to do with you."

"Are you sure about that?"

"Positive," she replied. "And I noticed that you didn't take the check I left to cover the costs for the pond. And don't think, simply because you're here, that I—"

She didn't get to say anything more because suddenly she was in his arms and he was kissing her. No finesse, no soft seduction. Just a hard, passionate kiss that should have infuriated her—but instead it curled her toes and unleashed a fire in her belly that could have sent them both up in flames.

And then he released her just as quickly, color slashing his cheeks, his breathing ragged. "Sometimes you talk way too much."

Nicola glared at him. "I officially hate you. And

stop sending me flowers and candy. And don't kiss me again… I don't like it."

"Liar," he shot back. "I think you're really turned on right now."

Nicola stormed across the room, then headed down the hallway and opened the front door. She knew he would follow, and she made a dramatic gesture, ushering him outside.

"Thank you for watching the boys. Good night."

He lingered in the doorway. "God, you're beautiful when you're angry."

"Go to hell."

He laughed softly. "I've missed you."

"Well, I haven't missed you," she shot back, lying through her teeth. Because she had missed him like crazy.

"I could stay for a while. We could talk," he said and shrugged. "Or make out." His voice flowed through her like fine whiskey.

His audacity was astounding. "I'm not in the market for another one-night stand. I'm looking for real commitment," she reminded him. "And that's not something you can give me, is it?"

"Who knows what the future holds?"

"I do," she shot back. "I know my future. I know that you're not in it. I know that on Sunday I have a date for the rodeo with a very nice man who's not afraid of commitment."

His expression narrowed. "A date? I don't believe you."

"Believe it."

"I was hoping we could go together. I'm part of the medical staff for the event, but my shift is only for two hours in the afternoon. I know the boys want to watch the fireworks, and I thought we could spend some—"

"I broke up with you, Kieran. And I have a date," she said again. "Now, good night."

He left, and she closed the door before he was down the porch steps. Then she leaned against the door and burst into tears. God, how long had it been since she'd really cried? Forever. Not since Gino and Miranda's funeral. And she needed it. She needed the emotional release it gave her. She needed to embrace the grief and sorrow that came with it.

And she was still blinking away tears twenty minutes later after she'd closed up downstairs, and then she took a shower and dressed in her pajamas and went to check on the boys. She was just about to turn off Johnny's night-light when he rolled over and spoke.

"Has Kieran gone home?"

"Yes," she replied and tucked his duvet around his bony shoulders.

"Marco and I really like him."

"I know you do," she said and touched his hair. "Is that why you took my cell phone?"

He looked instantly guilty and then nodded. "We were trying to help."

She knew exactly what they were trying to do. "It's wrong to steal things."

"I know," he admitted. "I'm sorry."

Nicola sighed. "You also know my password?"

He shrugged a fraction. "I saw you put it in once. I just remembered." He dug between his mattress and bed frame and withdrew her phone. "I think the battery ran out," he said and passed it to her.

She looked at the phone, then knelt next to the bed

and said gently, "Don't do anything like this again, okay?"

"I won't," he said, his voice wobbling. "I promise."

Nicola ruffled his hair. "Good night, kiddo. I love you."

"I love you, too."

She said good-night, headed to the next room to check on Marco and found him fast asleep, and then walked into her bedroom. It wasn't Gino and Miranda's old room. It was a smaller guest room at the end of the hallway. She couldn't quite bring herself to occupy the master suite. In fact, as much as the house was lovely and well designed, it had never felt like a home to her. She stayed for the boys but knew she'd never feel as though it was her own. Maybe she should put the house on the market, start fresh somewhere. The very idea made her feel more alone than she'd believed possible. She walked into the bathroom to brush her teeth, caught a glimpse of her unruly hair, red-rimmed eyes and blotched complexion and grimaced.

How did I get here?

And suddenly, every yearning, every longing, every dream she'd ever had came rushing forward and fresh tears burned her eyes. Marriage, children, a career... things she'd once believed she would have, expectations she'd taken for granted. Now, those dreams seemed so far away...unreachable as the stars surrounding a distant planet. And she was sad...for herself, for Marco and Johnny, for the babies she feared she'd never have. Because she did want kids. She wanted a large family, she wanted Sunday dinners and picnics by the river. And she longed for someone to love her, a man whose arms were strong and whose heart was big enough for her, the boys and any children they had together.

A fool's dream, maybe. But she couldn't let it go. She saw her children vividly...with dark hair and glittering blue eyes. The image was overwhelmingly acute and made her ache deep in her womb. It was the same image she'd had since she was young. Because, in her heart, in the secret place where she allowed only dreams to linger, she'd always believed that she would have Kieran's child. Even when she was with Carl, creating a life together, planning a wedding and a future, the old dreams would occasionally resurface, reminding her that she'd already had her one great love.

And, for a moment, she'd gotten him back.

That was what hurt—the knowledge that they'd been so close to recapturing something special. Of course, the outcome was all her own fault. She'd known going in, when she'd spouted words about purging him from her thoughts, getting him out of her system, using sex to sate her old resentment—in her heart, she'd known it was a lie. A falsehood of epic proportions. The biggest of her life.

But on Sunday, when Alex arrived to collect her and the boys in his state-of-the-art minivan that might have impressed her had she not felt so desperately unhappy, Nicola knew she had to snap out of her funk and try and have a good time.

Because Alex was nice. Tall, fair-haired and handsome in a clean-cut, accountant kind of way, he was exactly what she'd expected. He had a good sense of humor, two well-behaved young sons, a good job, and he appeared genuinely keen to get to know her. Although a little younger, his sons went to school with Marco and Johnny and once they were all seated in the minivan, they headed off.

They arrived at the show grounds a little after four

and had to walk a few hundred yards from the designated parking area. The bronc-riding events had already started, and they watched for a while, before the boys pleaded to check out the variety of stalls on the midway. As they walked behind the kids, Alex chatted about his job as a surveyor and asked her about the restaurant and her family, and it was all very nice. They sat at one of the picnic tables and watched as the band set up on the stage, eating hot dogs and sipping sodas.

Yep…as far as first dates went, it was a good one.

Except for Johnny and Marco. They were clearly not happy with the arrangement. They weren't impolite because they knew she wouldn't have stood for it, but they didn't waste any time letting her know in private that they didn't want to hang around with Alex's kids or Alex.

Things got worse when his younger son Tim raced off and tumbled into an elderly couple carrying donuts and hot coffee. The child was scalded down one arm and, despite Nicola's attempt to run cool water over the burn, the boy was clearly upset, and Alex suggested they head to the medical tent set up near the bleachers.

And, of course, since the afternoon seemed to be going from bad to worse, the first person she spotted when they entered the tent, stethoscope around his gorgeous neck, broad shoulders superbly filling out his white coat, was Kieran.

Chapter Eleven

His gaze zoomed in on her the moment they stepped in front of the small reception table and then to Alex as he explained to the nurse what had happened to his son. Marco and Johnny couldn't have been happier, and they quickly skipped past reception and headed for him. But he was at reception in seconds, regarding them suspiciously.

"Is there a problem here?"

The nurse explained about the burn and, within a few minutes, the wound had been examined and treated, and Tim had a gauze dressing around his arm. While Alex gave a few personal details to the nurse and the boys picked out grape lollipops from the jar on another table, Kieran cornered her by the door.

"You're actually on a date?"

She shrugged. "I told you as much."

He flicked his gaze toward Alex and scowled. "Who's the stiff?"

True, Alex was wearing a shirt and tie and did seem a little out of place among the cowboys and horses and locals dressed in denim and plaid, but he was still a nice man. And Kieran had no right to question her about anything or anyone.

"I think that's self-explanatory."

"Where did you find him?"

She scowled. "He's a friend."

"A friend like I used to be, or a friend like I am now?" he queried, his voice little more than a ragged whisper.

The implication wasn't missed. "None of your business."

His gaze narrowed. "You really like this guy?"

"Sure."

"And he likes you?"

"Of course," she said irritably. "Why else would we be on a date?"

"To torture me maybe?"

Nicola stared at him. "Not everything is about you."

He shrugged. "Do the boys like him?"

"Why wouldn't they?" she shot back. "He's a nice man."

"He's not the right man for you," Kieran said quietly.

Nicola's glare turned upward. "And why not?"

He reached out and touched her hair. "You know why."

She got lost in his gaze, suddenly held captive by his glittering blue eyes. His fingers stroked her cheek and as she pulled away Nicola looked across the tent and met Alex's curious stare. He smiled, nodded, and then gathered up his kids.

She left Kieran and met Alex on her way out of the tent. He spoke first.

"I'm going to take the kids home," he said and placed his hands on his youngest son's shoulders.

Nicola didn't argue. "Okay. Thanks for…the ride in the minivan."

He laughed. "Will you be able to get a ride home?"

She nodded. "Yes. Thanks again. Take care."

She said goodbye with the vague promise to see him again. However, she didn't stay in the medical tent but collected the boys, ignored Kieran completely and headed outside, finding a spot on the bleachers where they could watch the bronc riding. She sat there for an hour, fielded a few texts from both Connie and Annie asking where she was and hid among the crowd like a coward. And she seethed. Because he had no right to question anything she did. One magical night together didn't mean he had a claim on her. If he wanted one, he had to give her what she wanted. And she knew he wasn't ready for that.

But he found her soon enough and squeezed in between her and the boys, who were happy to give *him* whatever he wanted, it seemed. He'd ditched the white coat and looked sexy as sin in jeans, checked shirt and jacket. He offered her the coffee he carried and she refused, staring straight ahead, watching some cowboy get flung off a frenzied colt and then get to his feet without a scratch.

The crowd cheered loudly, and Nicola jumped. "I wish you'd leave me alone."

He grinned. "No, you don't. And now that your date has bailed you don't have any excuse for us to not to hang out together," he said and grabbed her hand. "So, have you had enough of this bronc-riding thing? I told Liam I'd meet him and Kayla by the Ferris wheel in five minutes."

"You want to ride the Ferris wheel?"

"Sure," he said easily and tapped the boys on the

shoulder and said they were heading for the rides. They had moved on from the bleachers and were walking toward the midway when he spoke again. "The last time we rode the Ferris wheel together, I got to second base."

"First base," she corrected and called the boys back from running too far off.

He laughed. "I'm sure it was second base."

"First," she said again. "And it was a long time ago."

He nodded. "You look nice, by the way."

She glanced down at her jeans, bright red shirt, sparkly vest and high-heeled cowboy boots. "Thanks."

"I think I must have a thing for you in boots. But I like the other ones. You know. The black ones."

"Weirdo."

He laughed again, and the sound rumbled in his chest, making her heart skip a beat. "You know exactly what you do to me when you wear those boots."

"I'm not exactly the temptress type," she reminded him. "But I'm glad you like them."

"So, friends again?"

She shrugged. "I'll think about it."

When they reached the Ferris wheel, Gwen was there, hands on the stroller that held her grandson, Liam and Kayla looking on with pride. Strangely, Marco and Johnny declined the offer to ride on the wheel, instead assuring Nicola they'd prefer to remain with Gwen. And Gwen looked delighted by the prospect. Liam made some faintly crude remark that was meant for adult ears only, and Nicola knew she and Kieran were being observed as though they were under a microscope. She almost suspected that Kieran had put the boys up to staying behind but, before she could protest, they were both settled on the ride and it was moving upward. It was dark now and, as the Ferris wheel lifted them, the people on the ground became smaller. She waved to the boys for a while, until they lost interest.

"Everything looks insignificant from up here," she remarked and stiffened when his arm came around to rest on her shoulders.

"Relax, will you? I'm not going to pounce."

"Your family thinks we're back together," she said bluntly.

"I know they do."

The seat wobbled and his hand tightened on her shoulder. She wanted to brush his touch away. She wanted to stop imagining they were back where they used to be. Because that hadn't ended so great.

"Are you going to tell them that we're not?"

"Honestly, I don't know what to tell them."

She shrugged. "It's not like I want people talking about us anyhow. I hate gossip. You know, you broke my heart on graduation day, and everyone knew it," she said quietly, almost to the wind.

He nodded. "I have to live with it."

"You devalued everything we were that day," she said, her pain suddenly palpable. "I hated you for a long time."

"I deserved it. All that hate and anger, every bit. But time changes things, Nicola."

"Nothing's changed, Kieran," she said and shuddered in the breeze. "We're right back where we were. And I don't know if I'd have the strength to recover again."

"What if you don't have to recover?" he said. "What if this is exactly how it's meant to turn out?"

"Then I suffered for nothing," she said and shook her head. "Because I'm back here in the same place anyhow."

"Which is where?"

Loving you. Nicola's chest tightened, and she felt the words burn on the edge of her tongue. "Wanting you."

He reached out and cradled her jaw, rubbing his thumb across her bottom lip. "Is that all it is?"

Nicola rested her head against his shoulder and sighed. "No."

"Then that's gotta feel better than hating me."

"Sometimes it's the same thing."

"And if we're both feeling it?"

"But we're not," she said and pulled away. "We want different things."

"What if we don't, Nic? Let's just date for a while and see if we can make it work."

"That's the problem," she said, dying inside. "You need a backup plan. An escape clause. And I don't want that, Kieran. I want stability. I want—I need—everything. Not the easy part, like dating and making out and flowers and making up after a fight. I have two kids to think about now, and they also need stability. They need a home. So, I need commitment. Assurances."

"There are no assurances," he said flatly. "You should know that better than anyone."

"Because I've been dumped twice?" She tensed as the car swung, realizing they were almost down at the bottom again. "You're right, I do know. But the next time, I want to get it right."

He laughed harshly, but she could hear the pain underneath. "You want the impossible."

"Maybe I do," she replied. "But I'm not going to compromise simply to make it easy for you."

"Sounds like you're trying to make it easy for yourself," he said. "You're setting rules, making demands."

"So are you," she snapped. "Only you're doing it in your usual passive-aggressive way."

"Why? Because I don't generally let my temper get the better of me? And I don't dish out ultimatums? Isn't that how we broke up the first time?" He shook his head. "We were eighteen years old, and you were making plans for our future. Talking about getting engaged. It's no wonder that I bailed."

Humiliation coursed through her veins. "I thought we were committed to each other."

"We were kids, Nic. Teenagers who'd been talking about college and summer break. And then, all of a sudden, you were obsessed with getting me to sign on the proverbial bottom line. I felt trapped and caged like I had no other option than to end things."

"Trapped and caged?"

He shrugged. "I half expected you to tell me you were pregnant."

Rage and hurt clung to her bones. "That's why you broke it off? Because you thought I was going to try and trap you with a baby?"

"It crossed my mind."

"You think I'd do that to you? Even back then?"

"People do things…"

"People?" She frowned. "I think that's *your* past talking," she said, aching inside. "Because it's definitely not ours. I never lied to you or deceived you. But because of what happened with your ex-wife, now you think every woman will do the same thing."

"People say things to get what they want. And let's face it, you haven't exactly been transparent about this thing between us."

"What does that mean?"

"Two weeks ago, you said we should have an affair,"

he reminded her. "'Just sex,' you said. And we did. Then suddenly, the parameters shifted, and it wasn't just about sex. It was about something else…about you wanting what *you* want. You can sugarcoat it any way you want, but at the end of the day, it's still a kind of deception."

The accusation was obvious, and the hurt she felt quickly morphed into anger. "You think I've manipulated you with sex?"

He shrugged. "You brought another man here today, knowing it would bait me."

Nicola was furious. The audacity. The ego. The conceit. Like he was some great prize that she was secretly hunting, using her wiles and sexuality. When he had so many walls up, so much baggage about being deceived that he couldn't see what was right in front of his face.

The Ferris wheel stopped and, once the worker undid the seat, Nicola pulled her tote over her shoulder, jumped down and rushed off, wanting nothing more than to get away from him. Outside the safety barrier, she spotted Gwen and the boys, and Liam and Kayla close by with their son at the cotton candy stand. She was in no mood for company and quickly asked Gwen to watch the boys for a while, knowing they'd be safe with the older woman. She'd taken half a dozen steps when she felt Kieran's hand on her arm, and he twirled her around.

"Nic, wait up, let me—"

She shrugged him off, conscious that her nephews and his family was watching the entire exchange. "I was right to hate you! We are so over."

Then she raced off, finding solace in the crowds, her heart in tatters.

* * *

"So, that looked like it went well."

Kieran glanced sideways, frowned at his brother and then sighed. "Yeah, just great."

His brother laughed. "I remember when Kayla and I first got together. I don't think I slept for a month." Liam clapped a hand on his back. "You'll figure it out."

Kieran wasn't so sure. Every conversation they had morphed into an argument. Every admission seemed to make things worse.

"I'm not so sure."

"Well, go and apologize."

Kieran scowled. "For what?"

"Anything," Liam replied. "Everything.

He turned around and saw the boys standing beside his mother, looking at him with serious, yearning expressions. Looking at him as though he'd screwed up…big-time.

"How're you ever gonna get her to marry you if you guys keep fighting all the time?" Johnny said and pulled the hoodie over his head.

Kieran turned hot from head to toe. The kid certainly had a way of getting everyone's attention. He looked at his mother, saw she was shaking her head slightly and guilt quickly swam in his gut.

His family moved off, heading toward the main stage where the band was playing. Knowing the boys were very safe with his mother, Kieran headed back to the medical tent to collect his bag and make sure he wasn't needed any longer. He grabbed his belongings, quickly put them in his car and then walked back to his family.

His brother was seated with Kayla, and they were completely focused on their son. His mother was talking to the boys, their expressions serious. He watched the exchange for a while, seeing the way they listened attentively and were nodding. Gwen was a wonderful grandmother, just as she'd been a wonderful mother. As he watched over the boys he realized he'd developed real affection for them. The knowledge that he'd become attached to the kids so quickly shocked him to the core. For two years, he'd avoided feeling anything. Avoided people. Avoided relationships. The very idea of getting involved with anyone after his divorce had been unthinkable. That he'd allow himself to care for a child again was unimaginable. And yet, watching Johnny and Marco sitting with his mother, talking to her so earnestly, Kieran realized that he did care.

He cared about them. And he cared about Nicola.

He'd never stopped.

Not after graduation. Not during college. Not through medical school and his residency. And not even through his marriage and divorce. He'd simply tucked the feelings away, wrapping them up because there was no point in dwelling on something that was part of his past.

But the past was over, and he was very much in the present.

Kieran walked over to the kids and sat on the bench. There was a lot of noise around them. A lot of families. Some sitting at picnic tables. Some stretched out on blankets with picnic baskets. Some were simply couples, holding hands, embracing, sharing a kiss or two. Even with all the activity—with the midway sounds, the band playing, the rodeo caller blaring over the PA system, and the sound of children laughing and squealing—Kieran experienced an almost surreal sense of intimacy with his family in that moment. He looked at his brother, so happy and content with the woman he loved and their baby son. Liam had fought hard for his happiness and his family and, despite the difficulties they had faced, he and Kayla had pulled through and made a family together.

Kieran thought about Jonah, who was fighting so hard to *not* be a part of them, but who had agreed to help his newfound brother build the ridiculous fishpond with little resistance. And watching Marco and Johnny together, seeing their bond the way he had a bond with Liam and Sean, Kieran realized he wanted that same bond with his half brother. They were family. Blood. And he needed to work harder. To stop avoiding getting close. Sure, Jonah could be a pain, but Kieran knew he needed to make more of an effort to break down his brother's defenses.

Thinking about Jonah turned Kieran's thoughts to their father. He'd spent very little time with J.D. since he'd returned to Cedar River. True, Kieran had always been closer to his mother than to his dad, but he was man enough to admit that he'd steered clear of J.D. because he was ashamed of his father's past. His dad had cheated and lied and kept his son a secret for three decades…and there was enough deception in his behavior to remind Kieran of his own failed marriage.

Nicola had accused him of still loving his ex-wife. But that wasn't it. True, while he was married, he'd believed that he'd loved Tori, but it wasn't losing her that had broken him inside.

It was failing. *His* failure.

He'd failed at his marriage, and he'd failed the child he had believed was his son. Because if Tori had truly loved him and he'd loved her, if he'd tried harder, been more attentive, given her what she'd needed, maybe Christian *would* have been his. Of course, it was moot now. And the pain, he realized, *had* lessened. Being home, working at the hospital, hanging out with his family had helped ease the ache in his heart.

It made him see that he could feel again. And trust again. He could live an authentic life and not be afraid that it would all be stolen away. Sure, it had taken effort. But with effort, he grasped as he watched his family, came reward.

Which meant one thing—he needed to make an effort with Nicola.

They were good together. They worked. They made one another laugh.

And she'd loved him once…maybe she would again.

He sent her a text message asking her to come back to the picnic table so they could talk. When she didn't respond in a few minutes, he sent an emoji of hands begging. When nothing came back within ten minutes, he took a selfie with the boys. When she still didn't respond, he sent another selfie with the kids, only this time they were wearing the fake nose-and-mustaches that he quickly went and bought from a vendor on the midway.

Of course, the kids thought it was hilarious at first. But when she didn't respond after half an hour, their delight turned to obvious distress.

"Has she left us?" Marco asked, clearly upset.

Kieran cursed his stupidly in involving the kids in his scheme to get her attention and managed a smile. "Of course not. She probably can't hear her phone's ringtone with all the noise here."

"She has it on vibrate," Johnny said, and Kieran glanced at his mother and shrugged.

"Maybe she got lost?" Marco suggested, his lip wobbling.

"Or maybe she doesn't want to look after us anymore," Johnny said and nodded, as though he had all the answers. "*I* wouldn't."

"Does that mean we'll be festered?" Marco asked, clearly unhappy.

"Fostered," Kieran corrected and then cursed himself. "And no, that won't happen. She's not answering because she's mad at me, not you guys. She loves you both very much. And I'm sure she'll be back soon."

"If she doesn't, we'll have to go and live with Uncle Vince," Johnny announced. "Coz *Nonno* is too old to look after us."

"But I don't want to leave my school," Marco wailed and began to cry.

Kieran grabbed his hand reassuringly. "You're not leaving your school. You're not moving in with your uncle. You're staying right here."

"Can't you do something to make sure she's not mad at you anymore?" Marco asked and hiccuped.

"Sure he could," Liam said and laughed, ignoring how Kayla jabbed him in the ribs. "Nothing makes a woman less mad than a…" his brother paused for effect *"…diamond."*

"A diamond?" Marco echoed.

Kieran glared at his brother and shook his head, but Liam was clearly enjoying his discomfort.

"Yes," Liam said, still grinning as he wiggled the third finger on his left hand. "One that goes right here."

"Would you stop—"

"Oh, for God's sake," Liam said, clearly exasperated. "Just admit that you're in love with her and want to marry her and want to be a father to these two great kids."

Pandemonium broke out. His mother started laughing delightedly. Kayla admonished her husband. And the boys were suddenly jumping up and down excitedly and then began whispering to one another. Kieran shot to his feet, when without warning, both boys suddenly raced past him and headed directly for a large oak tree. Before he could register their intent, they were both swinging from a couple of limbs and then scaled up the tree about twenty feet.

Kieran strode to the base of the tree, ignoring the curious stares and whispers from several onlookers. His mother and brother were soon at his side. He looked up, and relief overwhelmed him when he realized the kids were safe. He and his brothers had climbed the same tree many times when they were kids. Which didn't mean they could stay up there. There was a lot of noise around them, and he raised his voice so they could hear.

"Come on," he demanded. "Get down here."

"Not until Aunt Nicola gets back," Johnny announced defiantly. "We want to talk to her."

"She's going to be furious if she gets back and you're up there."

"But it's you she's mad at," Marco reminded him. "Not us."

Kieran sighed heavily. "I'm not joking…get down now."

"Do you really want to be our dad?" Johnny asked, eyes wider than Kieran had ever seen. "Because that would be okay if you did."

"I want you to get down out of the tree," Kieran said tersely. "You've got five seconds."

Both boys laughed at him. "Now you sound like our dad," Marco said and giggled.

Frustrated, Kieran pulled his cell from his pocket and sent Nicola a text.

They're up a tree and won't come down. Stop sulking and get your ass back here now.

It took two seconds to get a reply.

On my way.

Four minutes and thirty-six seconds later, she returned. And she didn't look happy. She ignored Kieran completely and looked up at her nephews, hands on hips, chest heaving.

"What's going on here?" she demanded.

"We're *pro-venting*," Marco announced proudly.

"Huh?"

"I think he means *protesting*," Kieran supplied and came up beside her.

There was laughter around them, particularly since the crowd had grown. In fact, there were about thirty people standing around the tree.

"Protesting what?" she shot back, arms now waving.

"Their right to get what they want," he said and shrugged.

"Which is what, exactly?" she asked, her eyes narrowed.

"Me," he replied. "And you. Together."

Her mouth fell open. "What are you talking about?" she demanded and then looked up at the boys before he could reply. "I want you out of that tree, right now!"

"Not until you stop being mad at Kieran," Johnny said matter-of-factly.

She glared at him. "Did you put them up to this?"

"Of course not. But they want what they want."

"This is ridiculous. Johnny, Marco…climb down now."

"Not until you two make up," Johnny said and almost lost his balance. A petrified hush came over the group.

"Do something, will you?" she hissed in Kieran's direction. "This is all your doing."

"I wasn't the one ignoring the text messages."

She scowled. "I needed to be away from you. I needed to think."

"Are you about done?" he inquired and watched her, bewitched by her beautiful hair and pouting lips. And then clarity washed over him like a great wave.

"I'm done."

"Good," he said and grabbed her hand and then promptly dropped to one knee. "Then, marry me?"

Chapter Twelve

Nicola wondered if she'd stepped into a dream. Kieran was in front of her, proposing marriage. There was a crowd of people around them, who were now cheering, and she could hear Johnny's and Marco's excited whoops from their spot in the tree.

She tried to tug her hand away, but his grip was firm. "What?"

"You heard. Marry me. Be my wife. Let me be your husband."

Not a dream. A nightmare. "Stop it," she demanded. "This isn't helping."

He shrugged, still on his knee, still holding her hand, still looking up at her. "It's what they want."

What the kids wanted. Of course. Not what he wanted. And she knew he was saying it only to defuse the situation with her nephews. "But it's not what I want. Get on your feet this minute."

"You don't want to marry Kieran?" Marco said from his spot up the tree. "We thought you liked him."

She did like him. *She loved him.* And she was furious with Kieran for making a mockery out of her feelings. She twisted her hand free and stepped back, looking around helplessly, searching for an ally. Gwen was smiling widely and nodded, and then she glanced toward Liam, who winked at her. So, they were all in on it together. A ruse to get the boys out of the tree. She swallowed hard, grabbed Kieran's arm and dragged him to his feet. Of course, she had to play along, to make out like it was what she wanted, too. And afterward, she never wanted to see him again.

"Okay," she said and looked up at the boys. "Sure, we'll get married. Now, can you two come down from there please."

She heard cheering and clapping, but it was suddenly drowned out by the white noise screeching in her brain. Humiliation coursed through her blood, and she swallowed the heavy lump in her throat. While it was clearly a great joke to the O'Sullivans, Nicola hurt so much she could barely breathe.

"You gotta kiss each other first," Johnny announced, tottering on a thick branch.

Nicola's heart lurched. If he fell…if anything happened to either of the two precious children she'd been bestowed custody of, she would never forgive herself. And they needed to know she had their back and that she would do anything to keep them safe and protected.

She took a breath and leaned toward Kieran. His arm looped around her, settling on her hip, and he drew her closer, his intent obvious. Nicola looked up at him, her eyes burning.

"I'll never forgive you for this," she whispered.

"Sure you will," he said and inched closer. "You just agreed to marry me."

"I wouldn't marry you," she said on a sigh, his mouth hovering above hers, "if you were the last man on the planet."

"Wanna tell them that?" he challenged, his gaze darting upward for a moment.

Her denial was smothered by the soft touch of his lips, and the crowd cheered again. Nicola swayed, felt his hand tighten, and she sighed against his mouth. His kiss reminded her of everything they had once been to one another, of everything they'd rekindled in the past couple of weeks and then of everything she knew they had lost. Because they had no future. The kiss was just for show. His proposal was a joke.

Suddenly, Liam was by the tree trunk helping them down, and the boys were racing toward her. Marco began jumping around them excitedly, and Johnny gave a thumbs-up sign. Nicola pulled herself away from Kieran's embrace and hugged both boys.

"Don't ever do something like that again. You scared me!"

"We've climbed that tree a hundred times," Marco announced. "*Nonno* brings us to the park all the time."

She made a mental note to talk to her father about his activities with the boys.

"I think we should go home now," she said, grateful that some of the crowd had begun to dissipate. "There's been enough excitement for one evening."

"But we haven't seen the fireworks yet," Marco wailed and then pouted. "You promised."

"And people should always keep their promises," Johnny added. "Right?"

"Of course," she said. "The rodeo event will be finished soon, so we can go back to the bleachers and find a good spot to sit."

"We'd rather stay here," Marco said and rushed over to clutch Gwen's hand. "I wanna stay with my new grandma."

Nicola moaned inwardly. Things had gone from bad to worse. She was about to explain that Gwen wasn't actually going to be their grandmother, when the older woman spoke.

"I think that's a great idea. Let's go and find a place to sit so we can talk about how great grandmas are and how little boys shouldn't climb trees without permission."

"See," Kieran said as Gwen walked back to the picnic table with both children. "All fixed."

"I really hate you right now."

His mouth curved at the edges. "Is that any way to talk to your fiancé?"

She laughed humorlessly, aware that they were now alone, standing by the tree. "I'm not going to marry you."

"'People should always keep their promises,'" he said, reminding her of Johnny's words. "Right?"

Nicola glared at him. "You know I only agreed to get them to come down. Stop being ridiculous. You don't want to marry me any more than I want to marry you."

"I don't?"

She waved a dismissive hand, torn between hating him and loving him, because he was talking about marriage like it was a casual thing, and to Nicola it was precious and something she had dreamed about. "They'll have forgotten all about it by the time they get home."

"Don't be so sure," he said, his blistering gaze unwavering. "They're terrified you're going to leave them."

She gasped. "I would never do that."

"I know that…but that's a child's logic. It's why Marco is so emotional, why Johnny acts like the tough guy. Those are their coping mechanisms for what they believe is inevitable. Being left. Being alone."

Heat filled her chest, and she glanced toward the boys. "But I'll never leave them. They're my nephews. My family. They're my children now. How could they possibly think I'd leave them?"

"Because when people are hurt, when they experience grief and loss that seems unimaginable, they get scared. And afraid. Afraid to…believe. Afraid to hope that something great is actually possible."

An odd expression came into his eyes, and for a moment, the tiniest of seconds, Nicola wondered if he was talking about the boys or himself. But the look was gone in a flash. And they were back to their usual stance… their usual wall of resistance.

"I should take them home and talk to them, reassure them," she said, almost to herself.

"It's not words they want, Nicola. It's actions."

She stiffened. "You mean, like pretending that we're getting married."

"I'm not pretending."

She made a disbelieving sound. "Are you saying you actually *want* to marry me?"

"Of course."

Of course. Just like that. He was about as romantic as a rock. "That's crazy. And impossible. Marrying you just because my nephews think you hung the moon is out of the question. I've told you before, I'm not in the market to be anyone's rebound relationship. Particularly yours." She inhaled a shuddering breath. "The boys are confused enough by what's going on between us."

"Are we back to the rebound thing again?" he shot back irritably.

"It's not a 'thing,'" she insisted. "It's the truth. It's

how things are because of what happened to you in your marriage, and—"

"My marriage is over," he said and ran a hand through his hair. "It's been over for two years. And if I'm honest, it was never much of a marriage to begin with. Something was missing, and—"

"I really don't want to hear the details about your marriage, Kieran," she said.

"You brought up the subject," he reminded her.

"Because I—"

"Because it's an easy target, I guess. Blame my lousy marriage for everything, and we don't have to face what's happening here, right now, between us."

"There's nothing between us," she said and grabbed her tote. "I'm going to tell the boys the truth."

"They'll be hurt."

She tilted her chin. "They'll get over it. They'll get over you." She took a breath, stronger, deeper. "Like I did."

She left him by the tree and walked toward the picnic table. Gwen must have sensed something was wrong and that Nicola needed space and time alone with her nephews because she gave her a gentle smile and patted her arm and then walked off to stand near Liam and Kayla, who were huddled close together and keeping a discreet distance.

"Boys, we need to talk," she said as she sat down and grabbed each of their hands, squeezing them gently. "I want to make something very clear to both of you. You are the most important thing in the world to me, and I'll never leave you. We're a family, and we'll always be together."

Marco's bottom lip did its familiar wobble. "We were a family with Mommy and Daddy, and they left us."

"I know," she said gently, her insides aching. "They had an accident, and they died. And it's okay to be sad about that. It's okay to cry sometimes."

"But not all the time," Johnny said and elbowed his brother in the ribs.

Nicola smiled, her heart breaking. "No, not all the time. But sometimes. And we should think about them and talk about them and always remember how special they were and how much they both loved you guys. But we have to make a new family, just the three of us."

"What about Kieran?" Marco asked. "Isn't he gonna be part of our family, too?"

Johnny rolled his eyes. "They just said that to get us out of the tree—right?"

Nicola couldn't deny it. "I don't think we should—"

"But he wants to marry you," Marco said, his face pained. "He said so."

"When two people like each other, they should get married," Johnny said and shrugged. "It makes sense."

"And he's building us a fishpond, and he put up the basketball hoop, and he fixed my hand when I got the fishhook in it," Marco added. "And he's taking us fishing soon so I won't be afraid of the water anymore. He must like us to do all that. Is it because he didn't have a diamond?" Marco asked and jumped up. "Because he could get one."

Dazed, Nicola shook her head. "A diamond? What are you talking about?"

"For right here," Marco said and shook his left hand vigorously. "So you won't be mad at him anymore. See?" he said and peered over her head. "You just have to get one, and then she won't be mad at you anymore."

Nicola turned her head and saw that Kieran was standing behind them, barely three feet away, and he'd obviously heard the entire exchange. She met his gaze, and her insides contracted. He had an odd look on his face, something unfathomable, and she could have sworn there was a smile twitching his mouth.

"They know," he said and smiled. "You can deny it. But the kids know the truth."

"What truth?"

"Our truth," he replied. "They can see it…even if you can't."

Nicola sucked in a long breath. "I have no idea what you're talking about."

"No?" he queried. "Then ask them. They'll tell you what you're too scared to face. Kids are surprisingly direct that way."

Nicola got to her feet and moved in front of him, keeping a discreet distance from her nephews, but close enough that she could still see them. "Listen up, Doctor Charm. Stop using the boys to get what you want… whatever that is. I'm not interested. Not in you or us. You had your shot fifteen years ago and you blew it."

As she said the words, as she felt them leave her mouth on a breath, Nicola experienced an ache deep within her chest. Because, suddenly, she was seventeen again, and her heart was breaking. And in that moment, she knew she'd never really recovered from his rejection. Knowing he'd believed she might try and trap him with a baby back then only amplified that hurt tenfold.

He stared at her, meeting her gaze. She watched as he swallowed hard and then took a step back. "I see. So, okay."

And then he turned and left, walking off, his broad shoulders disappearing into the crowd.

Heat burned her eyes, her lungs, her skin. And she

couldn't breathe, couldn't think, couldn't do anything but stare after his retreating figure.

Stay and fight for me...stay and fight for us...

But he wouldn't. Because he was afraid to really feel anything. He could make all the insincere marriage proposals he wanted...that didn't prove anything. He talked about dating her, about their insane chemistry but, at the end of the day, the words were empty because they didn't contain what she needed the most. His heart. His love.

"I see that you did exactly what you said you wouldn't do."

She glanced sideways. Liam. The man had all the stealth of a jungle cat. He was beside her, and she noticed that Gwen and Kayla were now with the boys.

"What?"

"Mess him up," he said bluntly.

Nicola wrapped her arms around herself. "He's not messed up."

Liam gave a shot of humorless laughter. "He's about as messed up as it gets."

She shrugged. "You're imagining things."

His brows rose. "I know my brother."

"Maybe not as well as you think."

His mouth curled. "I know he's crazy about you and your nephews. I know that over the past couple of weeks he has actually returned to the land of the living. And I know that the only thing that's changed is you. So, ease up, okay?"

Heat burned her eyes and she blinked. "I don't know what you think I've done, but you are way off the mark."

"Didn't he just ask you to marry him in front of fifty or so people?"

Her back straightened instantly. "He wasn't serious."

Liam sighed. "Really? Looked pretty serious to me," he said and shrugged. "But if you don't love him…"

"But I do," she said quickly and then gasped, humiliated that she'd admitted the truth to Liam when she could barely admit it to herself. "I mean… I mean…"

"I'm glad. You guys belong together."

They did…yes. "Except that he left," she reminded him.

"Isn't that what you wanted?" he asked.

"Yes." She swallowed hard. "No."

He chuckled. "Well, looks like you've got some thinking to do."

Then he left her, walking back toward his wife and son.

Nicola remained where she was, aching through to every part of her soul, watching as Marco and Johnny hung out with the O'Sullivans as though it was the most natural thing in the world.

Five minutes turned into ten, ten into twenty, until nearly forty minutes had passed, and she realized she'd hadn't spoken a word to anyone. Weeks ago, her life had been about routine and monotony and getting through each day. And then Kieran had returned to town, and suddenly she was back feeling a whole pile of old feelings. And she also found new ones.

Like friendship.

And companionship.

Bitterness turned into forgiveness. Resentment turned into understanding. She thought about the kindness he'd shown toward the boys, and her heart ached. She thought about the support he'd offered her, the wisdom, the shoulder to lean on. Things she was sure she would never have.

I'm such an idiot…

Because she'd set rules. She'd made their relationship about sex and nothing else, when the reality couldn't have been further from the truth. She desired him, she wanted him more than she'd ever wanted anyone. But it had always been more than that. It had always been love. Even when she'd hated him, her love for him hadn't disappeared.

She'd wanted him to fight for them and had despaired when he didn't. But she was just as guilty of *flight* instead of *fight*.

She'd left him after they'd made love, she'd run like a scared rabbit because she was afraid to believe it could be something more than simple attraction. Because jumping in meant risk. And risk meant vulnerability. Risk meant surrender.

And surrender had let her down in the past.

Nicola let out a weary sigh just as the band started playing again. Gwen said she wanted to sit closer to the stage, so they grabbed their belongings and found a table near the dance floor. The fireworks would be starting soon, and the boys promised to sit quietly and share Johnny's gaming console until then. Liam and Kayla hit the dance floor for a slow, moody cover of a George Strait classic while Gwen watched over the baby and her nephews. Suddenly, Nicola felt so alone she could barely stand being in her own skin. There seemed to be couples everywhere, and she stood by the table, arms crossed, heart aching, wanting his arms around her so much every part of her hurt.

And then she saw him.

He stood on the other side of the dance floor, and the throngs of people seemed to do a kind of instant divide. He was watching her, and she couldn't have looked away if she'd tried. He took a step the same time she did, until they were both in the center of the dance floor.

"You came back."

He nodded. "We had some unfinished business."

"I know. But I wasn't sure if you thought it was worth fighting for.

"It is," he said. "Turns out, it's the only thing that matters. Unless you really think I've blown it for good."

She shook her head, trying not to cry. "You haven't. I was so upset, so angry, and...I think I just said that to hurt you."

"It worked."

"I guess we've hurt one another a lot over the years."

"I have more than you," he acknowledged. "I guess you owed me one. But I got your point, Nic."

"You know you make me crazy."

"Ditto," he said and smiled a fraction, holding out his hand. "Would you dance with me?"

She smiled. "No point in wasting a good George Strait song."

He chuckled and drew her close. "You know how I said there was something missing in my marriage?" he said and took her hand, raising it to his mouth and kissing her knuckles softly. "Do you want to know what that was?"

She nodded, in a trance. "What?"

His gaze burned into hers. "You."

Nicola's heart leaped in her chest. "Me?"

He took a long, shuddering breath, stared deep into her eyes and spoke. "You're the love of my life, Nic. You always have been."

Her racing heart skipped a beat, and then another. "Are you sure?"

"Positive. And this is not a rebound thing. This isn't

about sex, although making love to you is out of this world. The truth is I love you. I can't imagine loving anyone *but* you."

Nicola's world spun, and she pressed closer, feeling the heat and strength that emanated from him seep deeply into her bones, and she said what was in her heart. "I love you, too."

Kieran had spent two years in a kind of emotional wilderness, afraid to open himself up. Now he was feeling closer to Nicola than he ever had to anyone, ever. Her words filled his heart and soul. Her words made him feel alive and whole. They chased off every fear he harbored about intimacy and closeness.

The song ended and another began, and he rocked her in his arms, feeling her pressed against him, happier than he ever remembered being in his life. She swayed, and his hand traveled down her back, resting on her hip. With his free hand, he reached into his pocket and pulled out a small box.

"What's this?" she asked.

He grinned. "Where do you think I've been for the last hour?" he said and deftly flipped open the lid, exposing the antique diamond ring. "Marry me?"

"Oh, it's beautiful," she said with a sigh. "But where did you get it?"

"It was my grandmother's," he explained and kissed her forehead gently. "She gave it to me when we were first dating. I guess she thought I might have a use for it one day. So…is that a *yes*?"

She smiled and nodded. "Yes. One hundred percent yes."

He slipped the ring on her finger, and it looked as though it had always belonged there. "That looks good."

"Are we really doing this?"

"You bet," he said and kissed her mouth. "Let's go and tell the boys."

She touched his cheek and then gently moved his face in the direction of the tables. "Um, I think they might have figured it out already."

Kieran spotted Marco and Johnny standing with his mother, Liam and Kayla, and they all looked delighted. He laughed, looped an arm around her waist and walked her off the dance floor.

"So, when's the wedding?" Liam asked and patted him on the shoulder.

"No idea," Nicola replied and showed off her ring to Kayla. "But soon."

Marco tugged on Kieran's coat. "Does that mean you get to live with us now?"

"It sure does, kid."

The little boy grinned happily. "And does that mean you'll give Aunt Nicola a baby now?"

He laughed, seeing Nicola's embarrassment and loving her for it. A baby. A child with Nicola. Weeks ago, the idea would have made him run a mile. But now, he wanted it. He wanted the whole package—marriage and kids and sticky fingers and pet hair and chaos. He wanted to feel every emotion, every joy, every single day.

"I'll see what I can do," he said and kissed her.

The boys whooped and laughed, and his mother hugged them both.

Kieran felt the rightness of it though to his bones. Nicola had always been his. He had always been hers. The years they'd been separated slipped away, and now they were exactly where they were meant to be... together.

Marco was jumping up and down, and Johnny came forward and held out his hand. Kieran took it, and the boy unexpectedly hugged him. And then Marco hugged Johnny, and Nicola hugged them all, and he experienced so much love for all three of them he wondered if his heart might actually burst.

My family...

His family to cherish. His family to protect. His family to lay down his life for if he had to.

"I love you so very much," he whispered close to her ear, his throat tightening, his hands trembling at the realization that he'd finally found his home.

She held on to him, her hands keeping his steady. "I love you back. *We* love you."

And that, he thought as the kids laughed and he kissed her, was the best news he'd ever heard.

Epilogue

"So, where's your mom?" Nicola asked as Kieran grabbed her hand and walked her around the back of the house and through the small orchard. "I thought she'd be here today."

The boys were racing on ahead, searching for adventure. Or *misadventure*, she thought and grinned, watching as they circled a different tree each and laughed. It was four days after Kieran had spectacularly proposed at the rodeo, and Nicola had never been happier in her life. They'd spent time together as a family. At her house. At the restaurant. And he'd taken the boys fishing and Marco had felt safe and relaxed under Kieran's care. He was so incredible with the kids it made her heart sing every time she thought about it.

The wedding was planned for mid-November, which was just a few weeks away, but she didn't want to wait any longer. Neither did the boys. They insisted that she and Kieran marry straightaway, and even though she knew their request was half fear, half excitement, she wasn't going to disappoint them. Her dad had expressed some early concerns about their intentions but, in the end, he agreed that she and Kieran had been waiting for this for fifteen years—which was like an overlong engagement. Connie had stepped in to help with all the preparations, and Nicola was amazed how quickly something could be planned with the right people arranging things. She had a dress fitting planned for the following Tuesday, the flowers were ordered, the family's hotel was catering, and now they were walking around the garden, making final decisions on where the tent and reception area would be situated.

"I wanted to do this with just us," he replied and looped an arm over her shoulder.

It was a chilly afternoon, but Nicola was as warm as toast, wrapped up in his love. She nodded and pointed to a spot as they circumnavigated the house and ended up around the front again. "I think the tent should go there."

He nodded, looking at the flat lawn. "Good spot."

"And the band there," she said, gesturing to the left. "We'll have to set up a parking area, as well. I'll talk to Connie about seating arrangements, and you still need to give her a list of anyone you want to invite who isn't on the list we made up together."

He smiled at her obvious enthusiasm. "Are you sure you're okay with this happening so fast?"

"Positive," she said and nodded and motioned to the boys, who were chasing one another. "They're so excited. And they adore you. So do I," she added and pressed close into him. He was warm and welcoming and familiar, and she looped her arms around his waist beneath his sheepskin-lined jacket, snuggling close. "Is Sean coming back for the wedding?" she asked.

He nodded. "He's agreed to be a groomsman alongside Jonah."

"That's good," she said. "And I'm so happy your nieces will be flower girls."

"It was good of you to include them. It would have meant a lot to Liz. And Grady and Marissa were delighted for the girls to be a part of the day. And of course, Liam is the best man."

She shook her head playfully. "Not a chance. You're the best man I've ever known."

He laughed, and the sound warmed her blood. "That's very sweet."

"It's the truth," she said, loving him, needing him, wanting him. "Every moment I spend with you I realize that more and more. I love you, Kieran. And it feels so good to say. So good to feel."

He turned her around, grasped her chin and titled her face to meet him. "No regrets."

"Not one," she said on a sigh. "Only that we didn't do this a long time ago."

He kissed her mouth softly, lingering at the corner, his hand coming around her nape seductively, with a promise of what was to come. "I guess we both had to work out a way to get back to one another. But I promise you, Nic, I will love you and cherish you and always keep you in my heart. And whatever we face, we'll do it together."

She sighed and touched his face. "That's what you should say," she said and smiled when he frowned a little. "Your vows…you said you were wondering what you should say. And *that* was perfect."

He kissed her again, deeper, with every ounce of love she knew he felt. "Okay."

"I feel like I'm dreaming. It's all happened so fast. So much change."

He grasped her chin. "Feel like a bit more—hmm?"

"Huh?"

"Change," he explained and smiled. "Well, you see, my mom is moving out."

"Moving out?"

"From here. She wants to live in town. She has friends there, and she reckons this place is too big to have only her rattling around in it. So, I was thinking, this would be a great place to raise our family."

Nicola's heart stopped. *Their family.* They were the sweetest words she had ever heard.

"Live *here*?"

She looked at the boys, still racing around, laughing and having a wonderful time. They looked so happy. She glanced around, taking in the huge home, the perfectly landscaped gardens, the wide driveway, the barn and stables, the acres of pastures crisscrossed with white fences. From the orchard to the pool to the tennis court around the back, the place reeked of luxury and wealth.

But that was not what drew her to it. It was a home. Despite their own rocky marriage, Gwen and J. D. O'Sullivan had raised their children here with love, and it showed in every nook, every garden, every hall and every room in the big house. And Nicola could think of nothing better than raising a family in such a place.

She smiled warmly. "Yes."

"Yes?" He grinned. "No argument? No discussion?"

"Nope," she replied. "I think it's a great idea."

"Really? But your brother's house..."

"I should never have stayed there," she admitted. "You were right when you said it was filled with memories of all they had lost. In a way, I was selfish, thinking about how it would be easier for me by living there, not disrupting the boys' routine."

"You're the least selfish person I've ever met," he said gently.

"I'm not, really," she said and sighed. "Being surrounded by the memory of Gino and Miranda, their belongings, even driving their old car. I took the easy way out. But no more. I want to sell the house and put the money into a trust for the kids."

"Of course," he said gently. "And how about we find a spot here on the ranch and create a kind of memorial for them, somewhere the boys can have a special place to remember their parents."

Tears plumped at the corners of her eyes. "That's a lovely idea. And I would love to live here with you and raise the boys in this wonderful place. Just the four of us. Or five or six," she added. "In case anyone else comes along."

She watched as he swallowed hard, his smooth throat closing over. She knew it was a hard subject for him. Maybe the hardest they would face. Finally, he spoke. "You really want children?"

She nodded. "Yes… I'd like to have a child with you. Are you okay with that?"

He squeezed her hand. "Even though I can't guarantee that I won't be insecure at times?"

She knew how hard it was for him to feel and say that. And she loved him more for having the courage to face his fears. "So…that's a *yes*? We'll have kids if we can?"

He smiled. "Well, I did promise Marco I would give you a baby…and a person should always keep their promises."

She laughed, loving him so much she could barely breathe. "I can't wait to marry you and have your baby and live in this beautiful house."

He hauled her into his arms and twirled her around.

She laughed and, once her feet were back on the ground, she nodded and called for the boys to come closer. "You tell the boys. I mean, they already think you hung the moon. Once they find out they'll be living here permanently, they'll think you've given them the stars, as well."

He called the boys over and began to tell them about the house. And Nicola knew she had all she'd ever dreamed of. And more. They were a family. Which was everything.

* * * * *

MILLS & BOON

Coming next month

RESCUING THE ROYAL RUNAWAY BRIDE
Ally Blake

"Look," Will said, stopping to clear his throat. "I'm heading towards court so I can give you a lift if you're heading in that direction. Or drop you...wherever it is you are going." On foot. Through muddy countryside. In what had probably been some pretty fancy shoes, considering the party dress that went with them. From what he had seen there was nothing for miles bar the village behind him, and the palace some distance ahead. "Were you heading to the wedding, then?"

It was a simple enough question, but the girl looked as if she'd been slapped. Laughter gone, colour gone, dark tears suddenly wobbled precariously in the corners of her eyes.

She recovered quickly, dashing a finger under each eye, sniffing and taking a careful step back. "No. No, thanks. I'm... I'll be fine. You go ahead. Thank you, though."

With that she lifted her dress, turned her back on him and picked her way across the road, slipping a little, tripping on her skirt more.

If the woman wanted to make her own way, dressed and shod as she was, then who was he to argue? He almost convinced himself too. Then he caught the moment she glanced towards the palace, hidden some-where on the other side of the trees, and decidedly changed tack so that she was heading in the absolute opposite direction.

And, like the snick of a well-oiled combination lock, everything suddenly clicked into place.

The dress with its layers of pink lace, voluminous skirt and hints of rose-gold thread throughout.

The pink train—was that what they called it?—was trailing in the mud behind her.

Will's gaze dropped to her left hand clenched around a handful of skirt. A humungous pink rock the size of a thumbnail in a thin rose-gold band glinted thereupon.

He'd ribbed Hugo enough through school when the guy had been forced to wear the sash of his country at formal events: pink and rose-gold—the colours of the Vallemontian banner.

Only one woman in the country would be wearing a gown in those colours today.

If Will wasn't mistaken, he'd nearly run down one Mercedes Gray Leonine.

Who—instead of spending her last moments as a single woman laughing with her bridesmaids and hugging her family before heading off to marry the estimable Prince Alessandro Hugo Giordano and become a princess of Vallemont—was making a desperate, muddy, shoeless run for the hills.

Perfect.

Continue reading
RESCUING THE ROYAL RUNAWAY BRIDE
Ally Blake

Available next month
www.millsandboon.co.uk

LET'S TALK
Romance

For exclusive extracts, competitions
and special offers, find us online: